LESLIE SCOTT

BLACK BONANZA

CENTER POINT LARGE PRINT
THORNDIKE, MAINE

One

"After dark, walk in the middle of the street and tote guns. And tote 'em in your hands, not on your hips, so everybody can see you're loaded."

That was the advice given by Beaumont's town marshal to the oil town's citizens. And it was advice worth heeding, for Beaumont was as wild and woolly a town as Texas ever produced, which is saying considerable.

Roughs, toughs, petty thieves, thieves that were not petty, lease gamblers and gamblers who worked with the pasteboards and the galloping dominoes, spurious stock promoters, soldiers of fortune, ladies of the evening, professional gun slingers, and all the riffraff, male and female, seeking the easy pickings of an oil-mad crowd, swarmed over Beaumont and prospered.

Although it was a helldorado the equal of any gold rush town of the West, Beaumont did not owe its inception to a "strike." Long before Anthony F. Lucas drilled his first well three miles to the south, Beaumont was a thriving community. About 1825, Noah and Nancy Tevis, immigrants from Tennessee, built a cabin on the banks of the Neches River. A little settlement grew up around the original cabin and was known as Tevis Bluff. With mink, raccoon, beaver, opossum, and muskrat swarming in the rivers and bayous of the section, a flourishing trapping industry was soon established.

The possibilities of the site attracted the attention of Henry Millard of the Thomas B. Huling Company, a land-purchasing group. In 1835, Millard bought fifty acres of land from Noah Tevis and laid out a town which was named Beaumont. The town grew swiftly and in 1838 replaced Jefferson as the county seat.

By 1840, Beaumont was a really going concern and busily engaged in the development of a lumber industry. Shingles, always in demand, were first made by sawing logs into shingle lengths, splitting the cuts into proper thicknesses and thinning the edges with a drawing knife. Meanwhile southern planters and cattlemen were settling in the vicinity and producing cattle, cotton and sugar cane.

With the river fifty feet deep at the end of Main Street, Gulf schooners and side-wheel river boats nosed their way through Sabine Pass and up the Neches River and carried on a busy traffic in cotton, cattle and shingles, early laying the foundation of the town's importance as a port.

Not long after the founding of Beaumont, a row was started in the section by gentlemen who decided that a profitable crop of rice could be grown on the fat lowlands. The cattlemen, who

6

owned much of the rangeland and claimed much more, had no objections to rice, but they bitterly resented the coming of barbed wire to cow country and frequently registered their protests with six-shooters. The rice growers explained their side of the argument with others of similar calibre, and powdersmoke mingled with the wood smoke of Beaumont's sawmills.

After a period of hectic disagreement punctuated by the burning of buildings, the poisoning of waterholes and folks shot from ambush, a truce was established. The rice growers prospered. Irrigation ditches were dug, pumping plants installed and a steady increase in acreage planted, until before the turn of the century more than six thousand acres of rice were under cultivation, and rice was pushing lumber and cattle as the region's leading industry.

Withal, Beaumont was just a bustling, prosperous and cheerful piny woods community until Tony Lucas drilled a hole in the prairie three miles to the south.

The drill was down nearly twelve hundred feet when the sand formation gave way to a rock stratum and the crew shut down to change the bit and sink a new casing. Neither Lucas nor the experienced members of his crew were unduly optimistic over the oil signs, but suddenly, almost without warning, there was a deafening roar. Tons of pipe were projected through the rig floor, up and out of the hole and high into the air. *Spindletop was in!*

Beaumont sprang up with a roar like that of a tiger scenting meat. The clock that had been drowsily ticking off the minutes and the hours spun around to strike high noon while the sun was still rising. Time ceased to have any meaning. Day lasted twenty-four hours as far as Beaumont was concerned, for the town never slept. Business establishments threw away the keys to their doors; why bother with keys when the doors were never closed! Beaumont became a city literally "in bonanza" almost overnight. Prices soared, food became scarce. Lodgings were not to be had at any price. Men slept in tents or under the stars, the lucky ones with blankets, the majority without. The wild spirit of recklessness infected even staid old-timers. Men who hadn't carried a gun for years took to packin' 'em. To be without hardware rendered one as conspicuous as to be without pants.

Down on the prairie storage tanks were built. The ponderous "walking beams" of the rigs rose and fell and bits chugged and thudded as more wells were drilled. Husky men in greasy overalls drilled for "black gold."

Everybody's pockets were full of oil stocks, most of them not worth anything. Parcels of land changed hands at fabulous prices, changed again for still more fabulous sums. Speculators bought

8

feverishly in the morning, sold just as feverishly in the afternoon, and bitterly regretted selling before dark, when some wild rumor started prices soaring again. The workers threw away with wild abandon, at the gaming tables, over the bars, into the hands of women, gold that was stained with blood and sweat. The rest of the world could go to blazes; *Spindletop was in!*

Two

Wade Rawlins liked Beaumont; but he didn't like what he was doing. There had been an aura of glamour and romance to dealing cards on a Mississippi River steamboat that was lacking in a Beaumont saloon.

In the cheap mirror of his hotel room dresser, he eyed his costume with disapproval. The long coat, britches, polished boots and string tie were funereal black; the somber hue of his garb was relieved only by his flowered satin waistcoat and the snow of his ruffled shirt front. He did not exactly approve of the face reflected in the glass, either—lean and brown, with thick black hair, straight as an Indian's; eyes a very pale gray and of a strange brilliance, the kind of eyes the Old West had learned to regard warily. They looked from under a steep prominence of brow, on either side of a high-bridged nose. The mirror also reflected a rather wide, slightly disdainful mouth, a cleft chin and a lean, powerful jaw.

Truly a saturnine face, cold and dark and unlovely, Rawlins thought. In which, as in a few other things, he was mistaken. Ladies of the steamboats and dance floor girls appeared to regard it with favor.

Rawlins was slightly more than six feet in height. His shoulders were wide, his chest deep, his waist hard and sinewy. He was a good shot with a Colt .45—he usually packed two—and not bad with a gambler's gun, a wicked little double-barrel .41-calibre derringer that snugged in his left sleeve and which a flip of the wrist could spin into his palm. He had a better than average education and itchy feet.

The education he had not put to much use so far; the feet he had put to plenty. They were the reason he was dealing cards in a Beaumont saloon.

Two years before, he had been old Roderick McArdle's range boss, and the Lazy V, McArdle's spread, was the best cow ranch in the county. But the feet wanted to go places, and Rawlins let them have their way. They did go places: to Chicago, St. Louis, Kansas City, New Orleans, among others. In New Orleans, Rawlins met a character by the name of Watson Doan, who had the gaming concession on a number of river boats. After a number of glasses of whiskey, Rawlins and Doan became quite friendly. The upshot of the association was that Doan, after watching the deft way in which Rawlins handled the pasteboards in the course of a poker game, offered him a job of dealing cards on one of his boats.

Rawlins worked a year for Doan, and enjoyed

it. Eventually, however, he experienced a desire to visit his old stamping grounds west of the Neches River. Perhaps the fact that he had just won a really excellent horse from a Louisiana planter with a penchant for trying to fill inside straights had some bearing on his decision. The horse, whose name was Flame, was a golden sorrel and stood nearly eighteen hands high. He had speed, endurance, and an equable disposition. So Wade Rawlins rode west and landed smack in the middle of Beaumont.

Rawlins looked like a gambling man, and Crane Francis, owner of the Alhambra Saloon, felt that he also looked like an A-one dealer. Francis had just had an argument with his head dealer, with the result that the dealer had left town hurriedly with a bullet hole through his shoulder. Francis offered Wade Rawlins the job.

Proverbially speaking, the rolling stone doesn't gather much moss; Wade Rawlins had only a few dollars in his pocket, so he signed on with Francis and took over a corner table where the game for high stakes held sway. The men who were on the way to being oil tycoons, usually occupied that table, together with a sprinkling of well-to-do ranchers and lumbermen.

Rawlins glanced at his watch; almost work time. He donned his broad-brimmed black "J.B.," left the hotel and strolled along the board sidewalk of the muddy trail that was called Main Street.

The street was crowded with a heterogeneous mass of seething humanity. Oil workers in greasy overalls rubbed shoulders with cowhands in gay shirts, Stetsons and half-boots of softly tanned leather adorned with jingling spurs. There were Mexican *vaqueros* in black velvet sprinkled with silver conchas, humble *peons* with ragged serapes draped over their shoulders and hempen sandals on their feet. Colored men, their teeth and rolling eyeballs shining white in their black faces, wore a perpetual grin as they chattered animatedly in their soft dialect. Here and there was an Indian, beady black eyes slanting sideways in an immobile dark face. Now and then a Chinese pattered past on felt soles. Prosperous shopkeepers in sober black and heavy-shouldered lumbermen jostled one another. The air quivered with whirling words in many tongues. The clatter of boots, beat of hoofs, shouts of drunken brawlers and high laughter of women all rose up, like mist from a marsh, from the crowded streets of the dimly lit town.

Rawlins turned into a quieter side street not far from the river wharves and sauntered along slowly, deep in thought. His attention was attracted by a well-dressed elderly man who had just turned another corner and was striding purposefully toward him. He was perhaps ten paces distant when three shadowy figures darted from the mouth of a dark alley he was passing and leaped upon him. He fought back vigorously, but the odds were too great. A heavy blow caught him on the head and he slumped to the ground.

With a bound, Rawlins was beside the prostrate man. One of the robbers whirled and swung a wicked blow at his face. Before it had traveled six inches it was blocked, and Rawlins' fist, hard as iron and with all his two hundred pounds of muscular weight back of it, crashed against his jaw and sent him whirling through the air.

But before Rawlins could completely regain his balance, a second of the attackers had ducked the blow he launched and closed with him. He was a big man, almost as tall and heavier than the dealer, and he seemed to be made of steel wires. He gripped Rawlins around the waist and nearly swung him off his feet. Back and forth they wrestled furiously, the third robber dodging about and trying to get in a blow. Then Rawlins' cupped hands caught his adversary's chin, snapped his head back and broke his hold. And this time he didn't duck quickly enough; Rawlins' fist caught him squarely on the cheek bone and sent him sprawling beside his companion, who was wobbling about on hands and knees and striving to rise.

The third robber dodged back, and Rawlins saw a gleam of metal. His left hand darted forward like the head of a striking snake, the derringer boomed, and the thief reeled sideways with a strangled cry that rose to a bubbling shriek. He thudded to the ground like a sack of old clothes, blood spurting from his throat in jets; his limbs flopped grotesquely for a moment, stiffened and were still. Rawlins flashed his right-hand Colt from its holster and sent two shots screeching after them. A wailing curse echoed the reports, but the thud of boots continued on down the alley. Rawlins holstered the Colt, slipped a fresh cartridge into the derringer and flipped it back into his sleeve. He turned to the victim of the attack, who was sitting up, rubbing his head and looking dazed.

"You all right, sir?" he asked.

"Yes, yes," the other replied. "Just a glancing blow on the head, and I've got a hard skull. Your hand, please."

Rawlins helped him to rise and steadied him on his feet. He was far from being a short man, but he had to raise his shrewd, keen eyes a little to meet Rawlins' steady gray eyes. He glanced at the man on the ground, whose throat had been ripped open by the slug from the derringer.

"My God!" he exclaimed. "You killed him!"

"Looks sort of that way," Rawlins conceded. "Come on; let's get out of here."

The other hesitated, still staring at the body. "But what about him?" he asked.

"Oh, the town marshal will find him sooner or later and pack him off," Rawlins answered.

16

"Dead men in the streets of Beaumont are not so uncommon as to create much comment. Let's go before somebody who heard the shooting comes along to investigate."

The other turned to face him. "Son, what's your name?" he asked. "Mine's Gates—John Warne Gates—and I'm very much in your debt."

Rawlins' face did not change expression, although he instantly recognized the name as that of the noted financier, sometimes known as "Bet-a-Million" Gates, who was taking an active interest in Spindletop oil. He merely supplied his own name and said, as they shook hands:

"This town is overrun by Border scum like that, and honest men have to stick together or they'll get the whip hand. Let's go, sir. I think I hear some folks headed this way."

"Right," said Gates. "I feel the need of a drink and hope you'll join me. Where's a good place?"

"The Alhambra, where I work, right around on Pearl Street, is as good as any and safer than most," Rawlins replied.

"We'll go there," said Bet-a-Million Gates. "Not my first visit to Texas," he added as they turned the corner. "I sold barbed wire up in the Panhandle, in San Antonio and other places, when I was younger, but I never saw the equal of this place."

"A strike town of any kind is apt to be a bit salty," Rawlins answered.

"Yes! Yes!" said Gates. "But it'll quiet down sooner or later."

They entered the Alhambra, imposing with its broad expanse of plate glass window, well lighted and orderly. As they made their way to a vacant spot at the far end of the bar, Rawlins spotted Crane Francis, the owner, standing nearby.

Crane Francis was a smiling man with hard, watchful eyes, and the slenderness of a finely tempered rapier blade. He was an affable host, pleasant to everyone, not too pleasant to any, and Rawlins had noted that his habitual smile never seemed to reach his alert eyes which remained impassive at all times. His Alhambra Saloon was the biggest and best in Beaumont, and he had other interests he seldom mentioned. Rawlins had gathered that he was becoming something of a power in local politics.

To Rawlins' surprise, Francis instantly recognized his companion and greeted him with a respectful, "How are you, Mr. Gates?"

"Not bad, not bad," Gates replied in his peculiar jerky fashion, "but if it weren't for this young fellow I wouldn't be feeling so good."

Francis looked puzzled, but Gates did not amplify his remark. Rawlins quickly deduced that the shrewd financier thought it best not to mention his connection with the killing of the would-be robber. The killing didn't bother Rawlins much, but he appreciated Gates'

18

sagacity; complications sometimes did arise from such incidents.

"One on the house," said Francis, and moved away. The head bartender secured a bottle that Rawlins knew was reserved for the owner's private consumption and filled glasses to the brim. Gates raised his in salute and drained it at a gulp; the bartender instantly refilled it. The financier toyed with his second drink and shot quick glances around the crowded, busy room with its roulette wheels, faro bank, poker tables and dance floor where a really good orchestra played soft music. His gaze came back to the darkly handsome face to which he had to raise his eyes.

"What kind of work do you do here, son?" he asked.

"I deal at the big table over there in the corner," Rawlins replied, setting down his empty glass and motioning for a refill.

Gates' gaze grew speculative. "Somehow you don't strike me as being exactly the dealer sort," he commented.

"Perhaps I'm not," Rawlins replied. "I got into it sort of by accident. I suppose 'cowhand' would fit me better. I was range boss for a big spread in this section, but I had a hankering to see something else besides a cow's tail and started mavericking around a bit."

"Good idea, good idea," said Gates. "Good for

a young fellow; fits him to recognize opportunity if it happens to come along. Was that way myself when I was your age. Never hurt me."

His glance strayed back to the high-stakes table. "Straight game?" he asked.

"Absolutely," Rawlins replied. "Francis won't have any other kind in his establishment. Says it pays off in the end just to take your honest cut from each pot. Says if you rob some greenhorn for a few dollars, or even a few thousand, you won't come out ahead. Word gets around, and your legitimate business falls off, and sooner or later you have to move on. Francis says he's here to stay."

"Got the right idea," agreed Bet-a-Million Gates. "Play the game straight, whatever it is; play it hard but play it straight. I've had my chances to turn a crooked dollar, but I always passed 'em up. Some may say I was foolish. Perhaps I was, but I sleep well nights, and that's something."

Rawlins nodded. He glanced toward the big poker table, which was fully occupied, then inquiringly at Crane Francis. A negative shake of the head was the saloonkeeper's answer. Rawlins turned back to Bet-a-Million Gates, who was regarding his glass in a contemplative manner.

"Have a notion you should be in some different line from card dealing or following a cow's tail," he observed without looking up.

20

"Perhaps I will be, if opportunity offers," Rawlins replied.

"Make opportunity—if you can," said Gates.

"Work here every night?" Rawlins nodded.

"Be seeing you," Gates said, shoving aside his empty glass. "Have to go now, but I'll be seeing you."

"Walk in the middle of the street till you get to Main," Rawlins advised. "Do you pack a gun?"

"Don't know how to handle one; figure I'm better off without it," Gates answered.

"You may have something there," Rawlins agreed. "Go heeled and you're fair game for any trigger-happy gun slinger."

Gates nodded. "Be seeing you," he repeated, and headed for the door, his step unusually lithe for a man of his years.

Three

Rawlins dealt steadily until well past midnight. Then a relief man took over, and he sat down at a vacant table for a snack and a cup of coffee. The orchestra had also paused for a breather and some refreshment, and one of the dance floor girls strolled over and occupied the chair across from him. Rawlins knew her only as Audrey, for the Alhambra girls employed only their first names. She was small, but her figure was well nigh perfect. Her hair was red-brown, the red predominating, and she had sweetly turned red lips, a creamy complexion and astonishingly big dark blue eyes.

"Wade," she said, "I was sitting at a nearby table and couldn't help overhearing what that nice-looking man with whom you were talking said to you. Wade, he was right. You should be in some other line, instead of dealing cards in a place like this."

"How about yourself?" he countered.

Audrey shrugged her slim shoulders. "A girl has to live, and where else could I make as much money as I do here?" she replied. "Besides, the Alhambra isn't a bad place for a girl to work. You know how strict Francis is. But you've got a head on your shoulders and you should put it to some use," she pursued.

"You have a very pretty one on your shoulders," Rawlins smilingly rejoined.

"Oh, stop it!" she exclaimed, a note of irritation creeping into her soft voice. "I'm in no mood for flowery compliments. I'm trying to talk sense to you, and you're no help."

Rawlins realized that she meant it and replied soberly, "No doubt you and Gates are both right; I am wasting my time."

"Gates?" she repeated. "That name sounds familiar."

"John Warne Gates, sometimes known as Bet-a-Million Gates," Rawlins answered. "Chances are you've heard of him."

The blue eyes darkened. "Yes, I've heard of him," she said. "And he is right; you've no business here."

"I sometimes wonder what you're doing here," he retorted.

"Making an honest living," she answered.

"Yes, but sometimes I get an impression that you're all the time looking for somebody," he said. "Haven't got a stray husband mavericking around, have you?"

Again the expressive eyes seemed to darken, but she answered lightly enough:

"Nope. Haven't met the man I'd marry, or if I have, he doesn't know it—yet."

24

Rawlins laughed. She was refreshing.

"Think on what I told you, Wade," she said.

"I will," he promised.

"And do more than think on it; do something about it," she continued.

"Perhaps I will, if I get a chance," he conceded. He was mildly startled at the similarity of her reply to the one made by Gates:

"Make a chance!"

The orchestra started playing. Audrey stood up. "Got to get back to work," she said. "As you know, Francis pays well, but he insists on getting his money's worth. Don't forget, Wade."

She glided back to the dance floor. Rawlins' eye followed her trim figure and he shook his head. He still couldn't help but feel she didn't belong on the Alhambra dance floor. Her choice of words and the modulated tones of her voice set her apart from the other girls. And there was a dignity about her that they lacked. Again he shrugged his shoulders. He had things other than dance floor girls to think about. He finished his coffee and went back to the poker table.

The Alhambra was enjoying a big night. Every table was occupied, the bar was crowded, and so was the dance floor. Four times Crane Francis had emptied the till and collected from the dealers' drawers to stash away the money in his back room safe. There was plenty of dinero in that old strongbox.

It was nearly four in the morning when the row broke out. Rawlins' hands were getting tired and he called for a relief. Leaving the poker table, he sauntered to the far end of the bar, ordered a drink and got it over the heads of other men who blocked the mahogany. Leaning against the jamb of the back room door, he idly surveyed the crowded room. Crane Francis passed him with a nod, a plump bag in his hand, and entered the back room, closing the door behind him. And at that instant trouble broke in the middle of the saloon. A table went over with a crash, chairs followed it; there was a bellow of oaths and a wrestling, lunging tangle. Three men who had been sitting at the table appeared bent on murder or something very like it. Instantly the room was in an uproar that was deafening.

Still leaning against the jamb, Rawlins stared at the ruckus, his face wearing a puzzled expression; he had never seen so enthusiastic a shindig with so few casualties. No blow seemed to reach its mark; nobody went down.

The floor men dashed in, shouting for peace and order. They had no trouble separating the combatants, who continued to stamp and bellow in a manner that set the hanging lamps to dancing; it had all happened in about six seconds.

Suddenly Wade stiffened. Leaning against the jamb as he was, his ear was almost against the closed door, and he had keen hearing. He was

26

sure that a quickly stifled cry had sounded on the far side of the door, and the thud of something heavy falling. He whirled and flung open the door.

Crane Francis lay on the floor, blood pouring from his split scalp. On the far side of the room two masked men knelt before the open door of the big old safe, the contents of which they were stuffing into a canvas sack. They spun around at the sound of the door banging open and their hands streaked to their holsters. Rawlins went for his guns, and the ball was open!

Back and forth gushed the orange flashes; the room seemed fairly to explode with the roar of the reports. Ducking, weaving, Rawlins answered the robbers shot for shot. His hat spun sideways on his head; he reeled as his left arm was struck a tremendous blow, recovered his balance and pulled trigger with both hands. Then, two bullet holes through his right sleeve, blood trickling from his left fingers and oozing from his right cheek, he lowered his smoking guns and peered through the powder fog at the two motionless figures sprawled on the floor in front of the safe. He turned quickly to glance into the saloon, which was a successful imitation of bedlam. Everybody seemed headed for the back room, except three men who were just streaking through the swinging doors. Rawlins started to rush in pursuit, but between him and the three fugitives who had staged the phony fight was a packed mass of humanity through which a battering ram would have had difficulty cleaving a passage. He holstered his guns and knelt beside Crane Francis, who was thrashing about and cursing.

"Hurt much, Crane?" he asked anxiously.

"Head busted open; nothing more, I guess," mouthed the saloonkeeper. With Rawlins' assistance he sat up, rested his bleeding head in both hands, and swore.

Now the room was packed, everybody bawling questions and trying to crowd closer.

"Shut up!" Rawlins thundered. "Somebody get a doctor. Atwater, where the devil are you? Come here!"

One of the floor men shouldered his way through the crowd. "Pick up that money and put it back in the safe," Rawlins told him. "Burns, get me some clean bar towels and water," he ordered another floor man who had put in an appearance. "Stand back, the rest of you fellows, and give me room to work."

Water and towels were quickly forthcoming. Rawlins cleansed the wound and padded it to retard the bleeding. He probed gently around the cut with a dealer's sensitive fingertips.

"So far as I can ascertain, there are no indications of fracture," he told Francis. "The doctor will know for sure. What the devil happened, anyhow?"

"The hellions were hiding behind the door," Francis answered. "They grabbed me when I came in. I tried to yell, but one clapped a hand over my mouth. Then the other hombre belted me with a gun barrel and knocked me silly. Did you get both of them?"

"If I didn't, they're doing a mighty good chore of playing 'possum," Rawlins returned grimly.

"Good!" said Francis. "I'm feeling better."

Rawlins assisted him to rise and helped him to a chair in a corner of the room.

"Take it easy, now, till the doctor gets here," he advised.

"Roll me a cigarette," Francis requested. Rawlins did so, and the saloonkeeper drew hard on the brain tablet. The head bartender was hovering around him, ready to attend to any want.

The crowd had drifted away from Francis and was grouped around the two dead robbers. Somebody had jerked off the masks, revealing hard-bitten countenances nobody appeared able to recognize. Rawlins peered over the heads of the others at the contorted features, and abruptly a burst of sweat filmed the palms of his hands and his upper lip. He turned at a touch on his elbow. Audrey, the dance floor girl, was beside him, her blue eyes wide and dark.

"You come with me," she said. "You're hurt. There's blood on your face and your hand's covered with it; you need some attention, too."

"Just nicks; nothing to bother with," Rawlins protested.

"Perhaps. But even nicks should be looked after. Come on to the dressing room; there'll be nobody there."

Rawlins went with her. He was glad of an excuse to get away from the whirl and patter of voices and the glances that were constantly shot in his direction. The inevitable aftermath of the tremendous buildup of excitement was taking place, and he felt a little sick; the two dead faces had not been nice to look upon.

As Audrey predicted, the girls were all out on the floor, chattering their heads off, and she and Rawlins had the dressing room to themselves.

"Take your coat off and sit down," she ordered. "Good gracious! The sleeves are full of holes; this will take some mending. Help me get your shirt sleeve up."

The cut in his cheek was trifling, little more than a bullet burn, but his bared arm showed an ugly, ragged gash where the slug had ripped through the flesh.

"A little more to the right and it would have broken the bone," Audrey commented. "Hold still, now, while I dress it."

From a drawer she took a roll of bandage and a little pot of antiseptic salve.

"A dancer always has to be prepared for accidents," she quipped as she went to work on the arm. Very quickly it was well smeared with the ointment and neatly bandaged. For the first time, Rawlins was conscious of considerable pain in the member, but her touch was deft and soothing, and after several deep drags on a cigarette she rolled for him, he felt somewhat better.

"Thanks a lot," he said. "I'll bet you're a better doctor than the pill roller who's working on Francis."

Audrey smiled, a dimple showing at the corner of her mouth, but did not otherwise comment.

"Now I'd better be getting out there again," Rawlins said. "Chances are the marshal has showed up by now, and he's liable to want to ask some questions."

Audrey's expressive eyes widened a little. "You were justified in what you did."

"Naturally. I really didn't have much choice and could hardly have done otherwise if I wanted to remain alive myself; but when somebody dies, the law asks questions. I suppose they'll want to hold an inquest; it's customary in such circumstances."

"I see." Audrey nodded. "Leave the coat here and I'll see what I can do to make it a bit more presentable." She drew a sewing basket from the drawer as she spoke.

"You're full of surprises." Rawlins chuckled. "You sew, too?"

"As I said before, a dance floor girl has to

be prepared for any kind of an accident," she replied, biting a thread with her little white teeth.

Rawlins chuckled again and left the room in his shirt sleeves. Audrey's gaze followed him through the door; then she shrugged and bent to her task.

Things were back to normal when Rawlins reentered the saloon. The bar was again crowded, the games going full blast, the orchestra playing. In the back room he found that the doctor had already patched up Francis. An old frontier practitioner, he paid little mind to such trivial injuries.

"He'll have a sore head tomorrow, but nothing worse," he told Rawlins. "You can't damage that sort much with a pistol whipping. You okay?"

"Fine as frog's hair," Rawlins returned lightly. "I've already been taken care of."

The doctor grunted and began putting away his instruments. "Don't scratch that bandage loose and you'll be all right," he admonished Francis, who was relaxing in a chair and smoking a cigarette.

"I won't forget it, Rawlins," was the saloon-keeper's only comment to his head dealer.

The town marshal had also arrived and was looking over the bodies.

"Tell me just what happened and how you came to catch on, Rawlins," he said.

Rawlins did so to the best of his ability. "That fake fight was staged to hold everybody's

32

attention and drown any noise that might come from the back room, of course," he concluded. "Expect they would have gotten away with it if I hadn't happened to be leaning against the door."

"You did a good chore," said the marshal. "Things are sort of hoppin' tonight. Just picked up another ornery-looking specimen around on Milam Street. Looked like he tackled the wrong jigger; throat torn out by a slug. A Colt layin' beside him, but it hadn't been shot."

Rawlins nodded but said nothing.

"Well, Doc Petty will want to hold an inquest on the collection later today," said the marshal. "Just a waste of time, if you ask me, but I reckon Doc feels he should do something to earn his pay as coroner. Be at the office about eleven."

"Then you'd better go to bed now," put in Francis. "See you tomorrow."

When Rawlins returned to the dressing room, Audrey held up the coat with a satisfied expression.

"Hardly good as new, but it does look fairly respectable," she said.

Rawlins chuckled as he examined the neatly patched and darned holes in the sleeves.

"Looks better than it did before," he declared. "You're a woman of parts, Audrey." He thrust his hand into his pocket, glanced at her and drew the hand out empty.

"Thanks," he said briefly.

Four

Rawlins found he had a stiff and sore arm when he awoke a little after ten in the morning. Otherwise, at least physically, he was in very good shape. Mentally, something was to be desired. He was still struggling with the problem which confronted him, a problem that had not existed less than twenty-four hours before. How was he to grasp the opportunity that he felt existed in Beaumont? How was he even to recognize it when it appeared?

Convinced that there was no more sleep for him, even if he didn't have an appointment with the coroner, Rawlins got up, dressed a bit awkwardly because of his arm, shaved with even more difficulty, and repaired to the Alhambra for a bit of breakfast before putting in an appearance at the inquest. He found Crane Francis already up and about, his head bandaged but otherwise his usual urbane self. Francis watched him handle his knife and fork for a moment and said:

"You'd better take a couple of nights off till that arm gets back in shape."

"Thanks," Rawlins replied. "Very likely I would be a bit clumsy with the cards tonight, and that game is not one for a clumsy dealer. I think I'll take a ride."

"Once a cowhand always a cowhand," observed Francis. "Never happy unless you're forking a horse and—"

"And following a cow's tail," Rawlins interpolated, smilingly. "I'll always ride, Crane, but I'll never follow a cow's tail again."

"Not so sure about that," Francis retorted. "Wait till you get a whiff of sagebrush sometime when you're a long way from the range, and see what happens."

"Crane," Rawlins answered, "you must be psychic or have a touch of the second sight my old grandmother used to talk about. That's just what happened over in New Orleans. They were unloading bales of hay from a barge, and one had a branch of sage tangled in it. I smelled it and got homesick; that's how I happen to be in Beaumont."

"I once tried to get out of the saloon business," Francis reminisced. "A feller opened a bottle of whiskey in my presence, I smelled it and got homesick; that's how *I* happen to be in Beaumont." With a grin he sauntered back to the far end of the bar. Rawlins chuckled and rolled a cigarette.

The inquest was short. The coroner's jury complimented Rawlins for doing a good chore on the two robbers and 'lowed that the other varmint, the one picked up in an alley mouth, had his death at the hands of a party or parties unknown who had done the community a favor.

As he rode south by slightly east through the golden autumn sunshine, Rawlins observed the derricks that rose at intervals all the way to the horizon.

As he surveyed the frenzied drilling of wells and building of storage tanks, a certain irony struck Rawlins. Here was a working of the law of supply and demand in reverse, as it were. Everybody was buying or selling oil wells. More were constantly being drilled to be bought and sold. Here was a ludicrous resemblance to taking in each other's washing. You pay me for washing and ironing your shirts and I'll pay you for washing and ironing mine. The financial merry-go-round was getting exactly nowhere. Somewhere the galloping horses had to break away from the endless circle and straighten out. Then Beaumont's and Spindletop's real prosperity would begin. And slowly it dawned on Wade Rawlins that in this outlandish condition opportunity was waiting to be seized by the forelock; waiting to be "made!" *He* was going to get busy with the making. He quickened Flame's pace and rode on.

Down near the southwest corner of the present limits of the "field," Rawlins found the man he sought, garbed in greasy overalls like any worker, and usually doing the work of two.

Jason Abbot was short and broad, with eyes like splinters of sapphire in a piece of tanned and wrinkled leather, a mouth that was a narrow gash above a long cleft chin, and a broad forehead surmounted by a bristle of fiery hair. In the oil business he had started as a grease monkey; now he owned a number of producing wells and was drilling more.

Wade Rawlins knew him as one of the most reckless gamblers who frequented the big poker game in the Alhambra; reckless but shrewd, with an uncanny ability to read men's minds and intentions. Rawlins liked him and believed the regard was reciprocated.

Abbot greeted him with a greasy grin and a wave of a powerful brown hand.

"Taking a little breather, eh?" he remarked. "Well, one man's meat is another man's poison; I come into your rum hole for the same reason. The smell is about as bad as down here, but different. Light off and join me in a snack; was just getting ready to have a bite. I'll have your critters put in the stable with mine," he added, gesturing toward a squat, tightly constructed building just beyond the cook shanty. "That's a fine-looking animal; want to sell him?"

"No," Rawlins replied shortly.

"Don't blame you," Abbot replied. "I wouldn't sell one of mine, either."

In answer to his whoop there appeared a man who had cowhand written all over him and who looked as out of place in his environment as did Rawlins. Abbot interpreted the dealer's glance and chuckled as the man led Flame to a stall.

"Hired him to take care of my beasts," he explained. "I wouldn't take chances with an amateur. Chuck knows his business and has a way with horses."

Rawlins nodded his understanding. Abbot was a lover of good horse flesh and owned half a dozen excellent mounts. He would pay any price for a cayuse that caught his fancy.

The "snack" turned out to be something in the nature of a gourmet's dream. Jason Abbot usually dressed like one of his drillers, but he denied himself none of the creature luxuries that money could buy.

"Hear you filed a couple of notches on your guns last night," he observed suddenly. Rawlins nodded.

"Better keep your eyes open," Abbot advised. "The criminal element hereabouts is getting organized and won't take kindly to such inter-ference with their activities." Rawlins nodded again. Abbot was silent a moment; then:

"Heard too that you were hobnobbin' with Bet-a-Million Gates. There's a man worth knowing, he can advance your interests if he's of a mind to. I wish I could get closer to him."

"Perhaps you can," Rawlins observed.

The sapphire splinters sparkled.

"All right," Abbot said. "Out with it! You didn't come down here just for the ride. What's on your mind?"

Rawlins raised his glass of fine brandy and regarded it with the eye of a connoisseur. He answered Abbot's question with one of his own.

"Jason," he said, "how much oil have you sold so far?"

The splinters sparkled again; their owner chuckled. "None," he admitted. "Nobody's selling oil; everybody's selling wells. Why?"

"Costs money to drill wells, doesn't it?"

"It does, plenty," Abbot conceded.

"And how long do you figure you can keep on pouring out money with none coming in?"

"Well," the oilman smiled, "there's a limit. What are you getting at, Wade?"

Rawlins again countered with a question. "Jason," he said, "how much oil have you in storage and guaranteed production?"

"About a million barrels, I'd say offhand," Abbot replied. "What *are* you getting at?"

"Just this," Rawlins answered slowly. "I'd like a ninety-day option on those million barrels, with the privilege of taking an option on the next million you produce, at three cents a barrel."

Abbot regarded him curiously. "And what are

40

you prepared to put down to hold the option?" he asked.

Rawlins drew a deep breath and took the plunge. "Ten thousand dollars."

A long silence followed as Abbot turned the proposition over in his mind. He took a sip of brandy, cleared his throat, and said:

"Done! I'll ride to Beaumont tomorrow and have the papers drawn up."

"Your word is good enough for me," Rawlins said.

"Possibly, but if something should happen to me during the ninety days, somebody might take a dim view of a verbal option with nothing in writing to substantiate it."

"Guess you're right," Rawlins conceded. "Send for my horse! I'm riding."

"What's your hurry?" Abbot protested. "Stick around a while; I'd like to talk to you."

"Want your ten thousand, don't you?" Rawlins replied.

"I could use it," the oilman admitted.

"If I don't ride, you don't get it."

"Then ride!" grinned Abbot.

Five

Two miles after leaving Jason Abbot, Rawlins knew he was traversing old Roderick McArdle's Lazy V holdings. As he continued west he surveyed the familiar terrain with an interest he had never before evinced. Fragments of knowledge, some half forgotten, tumbled through his brain, and certain topographical peculiarities assumed a new significance. Once he turned aside to ride up a shallow draw for some distance. Where a spring bubbled from beneath a shelving bank, he dismounted, scooped up some of the sparkling water in his hand and tasted it. Yes, it was the same as it had always been: bitterly salt.

Squatting on his heels, he eyed the shattered rock that formed the bank. It was blue shale, and if it wasn't kerogen shale, it was very like it. But this was the only salt spring and the only outcropping of kerogen on the Lazy V Ranch he had ever encountered, and he had ridden every foot of the holding again and again.

A single salt spring, a single outcropping! Opportunity? Perhaps. But a hundred-to-one shot if there ever was one.

Squatting comfortably on his heels and drawing hard on a cigarette, he determined that, somehow or other, he *would* put it to the test. A gamble for a million! Bet-a-Million Gates had said, "Make opportunity!"

He pinched out his cigarette, retraced his way down the draw and rode toward the glory of the sunset, heavy with thought.

The Lazy V ranchhouse, shaded by gnarled oaks, was old. Roderick McArdle's grandfather, born in the glens of Scotland, had built it. Outbuildings and a commodious wing had been added in later years, so that it was as roomy and comfortable a *hacienda* as could be found in east Texas.

Several hands were pottering about the horse corral when Rawlins drew rein in front of the wide veranda. They recognized him instantly and gave him a rousing welcome.

"Where's your fancy duds?" Zeke Pettigrew wanted to know. "When I saw you in Beaumont last week, you were a gamblin' man for fair. Figured you were plumb finished with wool shirts and Levis."

"Not when I'm riding," Rawlins replied, smiling. "When I'm forking a cayuse, I'm a cowhand again."

"And that's some cayuse you got," enthused Pettigrew. "Light off and I'll stable him. The Old Man's inside somewhere; go right on in."

Roderick McArdle was a little man, lean and wiry. His ruddy face was framed with white bristles, and a line of white fluff fringed his bald head. His little black eyes snapped as they rested on his visitor.

"Well! well!" he exclaimed. "So the bairn's back from his traipsin'! Give me the grip of your hand, lad!"

As they shook hands, Rawlins experienced a mild wonder, as on former occasions, that the Scotch burr and idiom should have survived to the third generation.

"Sit down," said McArdle, "and tell me the tale of your wanderings."

Rawlins rolled a cigarette and regaled his host with an account of his adventures and misadventures during the past two years. Old Roderick chuckled often during the recital and evinced an intense interest in the doings of his former range boss.

"Aye, it's the wild and hot blood you have in your veins, lad," he commented when Rawlins paused. "But now you've decided to settle down."

"Yes, Uncle Rod, I've decided to settle down," Rawlins replied.

"Good! Good!" said McArdle. "It's glad I am that you aim to bide a wee with us again. And if we can just find a bonnie lassie for you, perhaps you'll stay quite a while."

Rawlins smiled. "I'm afraid I don't take more than a passing interest in the lassies, Uncle Rod."

"Aye, but the right one, the one and only, you

have not seen as yet," chuckled McArdle. "Wait till she walks before your eyes, and we'll see what sort of a tune you'll sing. But let's eat, and then we'll talk some more."

After a good dinner, Rawlins returned to the living room with the rancher. For some time they smoked in silence.

"And if you don't intend to ride the range again, what have you in mind?" McArdle finally observed.

"Uncle Rod," Rawlins replied, "I want to ask a favor."

Old Roderick looked alarmed, and his eyes shunned Rawlins'. "Tut, tut! what is it?"

"Money," Rawlins answered.

"I knew it!" sighed McArdle. "Cowpokes are always busted. And how much would you be after wanting?"

"Ten thousand dollars."

Old Roderick jumped in his chair. "Ten thousand dollars! Hoot, toot, man, you couldn't drink that much whiskey in your lifetime!"

"I don't want to buy whiskey, Uncle Rod; I want to buy oil." Rawlins grinned.

"Oil! Do your guns need greasin' that bad?"

"I'm afraid that much would make them slippery," Rawlins returned. "I'll tell you all about it."

He proceeded to do so, outlining his plan with meticulous attention to detail.

"And I believe I can guarantee you a five-thousand-dollar profit on your investment," he concluded.

Old Roderick said nothing. He slowly filled his pipe, lighted it and smoked in silence, his eyes fixed on space.

The suspense had grown almost unbearable when McArdle finally removed his pipe from his mouth and spoke.

"It would seem, lad, that you have become considerable of a gambling man," he remarked.

"Perhaps," Rawlins admitted, his lips a trifle stiff.

"And I was brought up to look on gambling as an instrument of the de'il."

Rawlins said nothing, but his mouth was suddenly dry.

Then old Roderick turned in his chair to face him.

"Wade," he said, "I've always kenned you as an unco braw and sonsy man who would make his mark. I'll do it. But, mind you, I ain't Scotch for nothing. I'll be looking for my five thousand, against the time when you'll be after wanting help again."

Rawlins breathed a deep sigh of relief. He had taken the first trick in his great gamble.

Six

Rawlins' mood was jubilant as he rode to Beaumont the following morning. He had Roderick McArdle's check for ten thousand dollars in his pocket, and a lot of sound advice in his head. Things were working out fine.

First, Rawlins dropped in at the doctor's office to have his wounded arm given a once-over. An examination showed the injury to be healing nicely with no complications in sight.

"Be stiff for another day or two, but it's coming along satisfactorily," said the doctor. "Just try not to get drunk and fall down and bust it open."

Rawlins promised he'd try to exercise good judgment and repaired to the Alhambra, where he sat at a table and smoked while waiting for Jason Abbot to put in an appearance.

Crane Francis was already on the job, making ready for the afternoon and evening rush. He nodded to Rawlins but did not speak.

Gradually Rawlins got the impression that the saloonkeeper was covertly studying him. The intense speculation in the saloonkeeper's gaze puzzled him, until presently an obvious solution offered: quite likely Francis was wondering if he were coming back to work. Well, he could stop bothering his head on that score; Rawlins had no intention of giving up his chore of dealing just yet. He would be on the job after another night's rest.

Jason Abbot showed up around noon. Rawlins waved to him, and Abbot drew up a chair and ordered food and drink. He glanced expectantly at Rawlins.

"All set to go," Rawlins told him.

"Fine!" Abbot said. "Soon as I down this, I'll be with you."

A short session at the lawyer's office, and the necessary papers were in order. Rawlins endorsed the check, handed it to Abbot and received his option. They returned to the Alhambra and had a drink to seal the bargain. Crane Francis nodded and smiled but did not join them.

After Abbot had departed, Rawlins approached the saloonkeeper. "One more night of taking it easy and I'll be back with you," he said.

"Take your time," Francis replied. "Take as much as you want. I figure you earned a vacation the other night," he added with a grin. "What was in that safe would pay your wages for a year and then some. I'd have handed you a fistful, but I know you well enough to know you'd have told me to go to the devil. But you can't very well refuse to accept pay for the time off, seeing I was the cause of you having to take it."

"Guess you've got something there." Rawlins

smiled. "But I'll be okay by tomorrow night."

Francis nodded and turned to the back room. "Little book work to do," he said. "Be seeing you."

Rawlins might have been surprised had he been able to note the "book" work that went on in the back room. It consisted of an earnest, low-voiced conversation between Crane Francis and a small dark-faced man with high cheek bones and quick black eyes. The little man left by way of the back door and a few minutes later entered the saloon by way of the front door. He lounged against the bar, toying with a drink, and when Wade Rawlins strolled out, he followed him.

Wade Rawlins' immediate destination was the Crosby Hotel, where he hoped to reach Bet-a-Million Gates. The Crosby House, as it was known, was the "pit," the "curb" and "exchange" of the oil industry. Everybody showed up at the Crosby House sooner or later, and the place was always packed. So the small dark-faced, unobtrusive man who sauntered in almost on Rawlins' heels attracted no attention.

Bet-a-Million Gates was in the lobby, conversing with several gentlemen, when Rawlins entered. He almost instantly spotted the dealer's tall form, excused himself to his companions and hurried across the lobby, hand outstretched.

"Well, well!" he exclaimed heartily. "My young friend! Have you come to throw out the money changers? Might not be a bad idea, at that. Seems you were sort of in the business of rescuing people in distress the other night; I heard about it. How are you? Glad you dropped in."

Rawlins was pleased by the warmth of the magnate's greeting, which was not lost on the other occupants of the lobby.

"Let's go to the dining room and have a drink," suggested Gates. "More comfortable than at the bar, and we'll have a little more privacy."

The head waiter steered them to an unoccupied table and brought their order himself. Gates twinkled at his companion over the rim of his glass.

"Something special bring you here?" he asked.

"Yes," Rawlins replied. "I wish to have a talk with you, Mr. Gates."

"Shoot!" the other answered good-humoredly.

Rawlins hesitated, hardly knowing how to begin. When he did speak, his remark was in the form of a question somewhat similar to the one he had asked Jason Abbot.

"Mr. Gates," he said, "I suppose it has struck you that everybody in Beaumont is buying or selling oil wells, while nobody is buying or selling oil?"

"Beaumont has the gambling fever," said Gates. "No time for such prosaic matters as commerce."

"True," Rawlins replied. "But oil must be sold if production is to continue."

52

"No doubt about that," Gates conceded. "Oil will be sold; must be, eventually."

"Don't you think it is about time for it to start moving?" Rawlins asked.

Once again the shrewd eyes across the table twinkled. "Just what are you leading up to, son?" their owner asked.

"Just this," Rawlins replied. "I have a million barrels of oil for sale, and a million more on tap."

This time the eyes opened a little. Bet-a-Million Gates whistled.

"I'm not often taken by surprise, but this time I am," he said. "You have a million barrels for sale and another million coming up, if I heard right. Is it tanked?"

"A large proportion is, with production ready to refill the tanks as quickly as they are emptied," Rawlins replied.

"And what are you asking for it?" Gates replied.

Rawlins braced himself. "Five cents a barrel," he said.

Gates nodded slowly. "Sounds reasonable," he said. "Suppose you start at the beginning and tell me all about it? You can hardly expect me to go deeply into such a matter unless I'm familiar with all the details."

Rawlins told him, omitting nothing. Gates listened in silence. The twinkle was back, however, when Rawlins paused.

53

"Shrewd!" he chuckled. "Shrewd, and taking a long chance. Son, I've a notion you'll go far. Tell you what I'll do. I can't promise results, for sure—but I'll have a talk with Jim Hogg of the Hogg-Swayne Syndicate. I happen to know they are quietly maneuvering to get control of all production possible. They'll have competition— Andy Mellon, Guffey, even old man Rockefeller, eventually—but they are smooth operators and they're moving fast. They've got ideas ahead of anybody else—plan to build a refinery, several of them, right here at the field."

Gates paused to sip his glass. A thought flashed into Rawlins' brain.

"Mr. Gates," he said, "where will they build the refinery, do you know?"

"Well," said Gates, "the best and most logical site would be slightly west and south of the field. I'm pretty sure that's where they'll build, for various reasons."

"And is their plan to build generally known?"

"It's certainly not supposed to be," Gates replied, "so don't go spreading it around."

"I won't," Rawlins promised emphatically. Gates shot him a glance, and his lips twitched slightly.

"But to get back to Hogg," he said, "I'll see Jim and have a talk with him. I consider your price reasonable and I believe he'll think so too, although, as I said before, I can't promise anything. Can you be here about this time tomorrow afternoon?"

"I'll be here," Rawlins stated.

"Good! Good! I'll see you then. Got to be going now. Very glad you dropped in. Been a pleasure."

With a smile and a quick nod, he rose and returned to the lobby. Rawlins finished his drink and left the hotel. The little dark man with the alert eyes also left.

Wade Rawlins wasted no time. He headed for the stable where he kept Flame, got the rig on the big sorrel and rode west by south at a fast pace. The little man watched from a nearby corner and then hurried to the Alhambra Saloon, entering the back room by way of the door that opened onto an alley.

Roderick McArdle was a surprised man when Wade Rawlins walked into his living room shortly after dark.

"Well," he exclaimed, "back the same day! And now what? Need more oil?"

"Nope," Rawlins smiled. "Figure I've got all the oil I need for a while. Something else I want to talk to you about."

"All right," said McArdle, "but come along and eat first. Cook's all set to beller, and I can listen to your harebrained schemes better on a full stomach."

Rawlins curbed his impatience; when old

Roderick was hungry, food and nothing else interested him.

The cook "bellered." Rawlins followed McArdle into the dining room with a resigned sigh. Once seated, however, habit asserted itself and he ate as good a dinner as did the ranch owner.

After eating, they returned to the living room. McArdle got his pipe going to his satisfaction and cast a quizzical glance at his companion.

"And now suppose you be after telling me what you've gotten into," he suggested. "What have you in mind now?"

"Something that will make us some more money," Rawlins replied.

Roderick McArdle smiled. He was not particularly interested in making more money—he already had more than he could hope to spend during the rest of his life; but he was interested in the progress being made, if any, by this surprising former range boss of his.

"You've found a market for your oil?" he asked.

"Yes, I have every reason to believe I have," Rawlins answered. "I'll tell you about it."

He proceeded to regale McArdle with an account of his interview with Bet-a-Million Gates.

"The way Gates talked, I'd say things look favorable," he concluded. "It would seem the

Hogg-Swayne interests are out to corner Spindle-top oil, or as much of it as they can, and they'd hardly turn down such an offer. I feel sure Gates believes they'll buy, and I don't think Gates is in the habit of making mistakes in such matters."

"Good enough," conceded McArdle. "Now about the other matter that has got you excited—what are you after?"

"Uncle Rod, that southwest pasture of yours isn't much good for cows and never has been. But now I see a chance to dispose of it at a good profit. I'd like an option on that stretch—I believe it's about forty acres."

"Why?" asked McArdle.

Rawlins recounted Gates' remarks relative to the refinery the Hogg-Swayne Syndicate contemplated building.

"That section is the logical place for them to build. I feel sure they've got their eye on it. If I have an option on the holding, I'll be in a position to talk business with them. Of course there's a good chance they'd come to you with an offer to buy, but you can rely on it they wouldn't make mention of building a refinery. If I tell them I know about the refinery I'm sure I can get good terms from them. See how the situation stands?"

"Yes, I see," McArdle said slowly, "and what you say makes sense. You appear to be doing very well by yourself. Going to cash in your winnings and pull out of the game?"

"I am not!" Rawlins declared decisively. "I'm going ahead and become something big, if possible."

"Anything is possible if a man believes in himself strongly enough," returned McArdle. "Very likely you will become something big, as you call it, but as to whether or not you'll enjoy it I'm not prepared to say."

"I'll take a chance," Rawlins answered blithely.

"Youth is always ready to take a chance," said McArdle, "but like the bairn who reaches for the candle flame, sometimes suffers burnt fingers. Well, well, as to that, time alone will tell. I'll give you the option you want, but be canny. You are dealing with smart men."

Highly elated by his success in winning over McArdle to his point of view, Rawlins rode away from the Flying V ranchhouse the following morning.

It was instinctive with him, no matter how engrossed he might be, to keep a close watch on his surroundings. His keen eyes missed nothing of what went on around him. Every movement of birds on the wing, of little animals scurrying through the brush, every message wafted by shadow or tree branch was noted and evaluated by the alert monitor in a corner of his brain.

It was this automatic habitual vigilance, plus a bluejay, that saved him.

Directly ahead, a long bristle of thicket flanked the trail on the right. To the left was the beginning of a slope that thrust up a petulant lip a foot or so in height at the trail's edge, leveled off for a score of yards and then dropped gently to the floor of a wide hollow. Over the edge of the thicket, a jay was wheeling and darting and squawking angrily.

The bird's unusual antics instantly focused Rawlins' attention on the thicket.

"Now what's got old fuss-and-feathers worked up?" he asked his horse. "Snake trying to get at his nest? He'd hardly have one this time of the year. Coyote fooling around? Not likely in broad daylight. But there's something in that brush he doesn't like. Somehow I don't like it, either."

He leaned forward, his eyes scanning the brush where the aroused bird swooped and fluttered. The sun was pouring its bright rays on the edge of the growth, causing every leaf and twig to stand out in strong relief.

Just in time, Rawlins saw the quick gleam of shifted metal. He was going sideways and down when the gun cracked. The slug yelled through the space his body had occupied the instant before. He hit the trail hard, rolled convulsively sideways and over the pushed-up lip into the shallow depression at its base. Another bullet plowed through the slight mound and showered him with earth. A third struck a stone and screeched off into space. Rawlins flattened out, hugged the ground and managed to draw a gun he'd very likely get no chance to use. He was on a very hot spot. The heaviness of the reports told him the drygulcher was using a rifle; sooner or later one of the high-power bullets would rip through the edge of the trail low enough down to find a home in his body. To attempt to scramble to his feet would be sure suicide. Nor could he roll away from the sheltering lip to a place where he could get a shot at the hidden rifleman. That also would mean death. He tried to inch along in the hope of outflanking his attacker but instantly desisted; to do so he'd have to expose a portion of his body to the other's fire.

But maybe the fellow didn't know that. A thrill of hope shot through him. Groping about, his hand encountered a lump of stone about the size of his fist. He managed to root it from its bed and cautiously shove it in front of him. He winced as a slug burned across the back of his neck; the hellion was getting the range. With a quick movement he chucked the stone forward. It struck the earth a dozen feet to the front with a soft thud and a spurt of dust.

Instantly the rifle cracked, and the bullet smacked into the lip just above where the stone had landed. Rawlins reared up, saw the wisp of smoke rising from the edge of the growth and sprayed the bush with bullets, whipping the gun muzzle back and forth.

A cry echoed the fifth report, a cry that crescendoed to a bubbling shriek and was chopped off short as by a knife. There followed a thrashing and wallowing in the growth that quickly ceased. Rawlins flopped down and drew his other gun, straining his ears for further sound.

None came. Nothing broke the silence save the fading squawks of the jay that had whirled high when the shooting began and now was drifting downward in tight circles. Rawlins watched it settle into the bush, took a chance and raised his arm above the lip of the trail.

Nothing happened. The silence remained unbroken. Rawlins hugged the ground and debated what to do. He had undoubtedly scored a hit, but maybe the fellow was only wounded and waiting his chance. The settling jay was reassuring but not a definite guarantee of safety. His flesh crawled at the thought of leaving his dubious shelter and becoming a clear mark for the possible muzzle trained in his direction. He was sweating profusely when he made up his mind to risk it, coming to his feet with a rush, gun jutting out before him, thumb hooked over the cocked hammer. He jumped a foot as the jay whirled up again with an outraged squawk.

Nothing else moved. Flame, standing a few

yards down the trail, cast a mildly inquiring glance at his master. Rawlins drew a deep breath and moved cautiously toward the edge of the thicket.

Just inside the final fringe of growth he found the drygulcher, and he was not a pretty sight. A slug had torn his throat wide open, cutting the great pulmonary artery. The dead face was visored with thickening scarlet, and from the awful mask his black eyes glared wildly. He had bled to death in a matter of seconds.

Rawlins had no recollection of ever having seen that blood-smeared countenance and scrawny body before. The dark complexion and high cheek bones hinted at Indian blood.

With fingers that shook a little, Rawlins rolled and lighted a cigarette. Gazing at the dead man, he debated whether or not he should notify the authorities at Beaumont of what had happened, and finally decided not to. By keeping quiet he might puzzle whoever was back of the attempt.

He shivered, despite the warmth of the sun, as he walked slowly to his horse. He had certainly never hankered for a killer's reputation, but it appeared he was well on the road to becoming one, the way things had been going of late. Four in less than a week! No argument but that all four had been justified; but nevertheless, through his mind drifted an old rangeland saying:

"A dead man don't make a soft pillow at night!"

Rawlins rode on slowly.

In Beaumont, he stabled his horse, went to his room and lay down for a few hours before repairing to the Crosby House and his rendezvous with Bet-a-Million Gates.

The financier was not in the lobby when Rawlins entered, but the head waiter hurried to meet him and conduct him to a table in a quiet corner, where Gates was sitting with a keen-eyed, pleasant-looking man about his own age. He waved a cordial greeting as Rawlins approached.

"Jim," he said to his table companion, "this is Wade Rawlins, the young fellow I've been telling you about. Wade, know former Governor James Hogg, who would like to have a talk with you. Have a chair."

Rawlins shook hands with Hogg and liked his looks. After drinks had been ordered, the former Governor turned to Rawlins.

"John has been telling me you have a barrel or two of oil for sale," he remarked with a twinkle of his shrewd eyes. "Suppose you tell me about it."

Rawlins told him and produced the papers that corroborated his statements. Evidently Gates had been briefing Hogg on the transaction, for he appeared familiar with all the details of the matter. He looked over the papers and nodded his massive head.

"All right, Mr. Rawlins," he said. "Everything

appears to be in order and your price satisfactory. We'll buy your oil, and the second million barrels when they are flowing into the tanks."

Rawlins murmured his thanks. "And there's another little item I have a notion might interest you, Mr. Hogg," he said. "I hold an option on forty acres of land slightly to the west and south of the field."

Hogg's eyes widened. He whirled to face Gates. "John, did you put him up to this?" he demanded accusingly.

"I did not," Gates disclaimed. "I merely told him you contemplated building a refinery. He figured out the rest for himself."

Mr. Hogg shook his head and said several things he had never learned in Sunday School.

"One Bet-a-Million Gates mavericking around is bad enough," he growled. "I'd fondly hoped and trusted we wouldn't have to put up with another, but now I'm beginning to wonder."

John Gates threw back his head and roared with laughter. Hogg grinned, albeit a trifle sourly.

"You win, Mr. Rawlins," he said. "We want that land and are ready to pay a reasonable price for it. Now let's settle the business before you pull another rabbit out of the hat."

The upshot of the matter was, after settling accounts with Roderick McArdle, Wade Rawlins had nearly twenty-five thousand dollars to his credit in the bank, with more to come when the second million barrels began refilling the tanks.

It struck Rawlins when he returned to work the night after his interview with Gates and Jim Hogg that Crane Francis was nervous and ill at ease; but Francis had been a bit jumpy ever since the abortive robbery, and he thought little of it.

Later in the evening, when he was having a cup of coffee and a snack, Audrey paused at his table.

"You've got the place buzzing," she announced. "You know there are no secrets in Beaumont, and everybody's wondering just what's up between you and Mr. Gates and Jim Hogg."

"Perhaps I'm trying to persuade them to sit in on the game," Rawlins smiled.

"A likely story!" scoffed Audrey. "I can see you drumming up trade for a poker table. I hope you plan to go to work for them," she added. "You'd do well with men like that."

"Anxious to get rid of me, eh?" he bantered.

"You know I'm not," she replied. "You're the only person of intelligence with whom I get a chance to speak. I'm only thinking of your own good."

"I gravely fear your notions of intelligence need a going over," he answered dryly.

"False modesty doesn't become you," she retorted.

Rawlins chuckled. "But it *is* nice of you to consider my welfare, and I appreciate it," he said quickly. He yielded to a sudden impulse.

"Like for me to tell you about what I've been doing?" he asked.

"Yes," she replied, "please do."

He told her in detail, and when he had finished, the blue eyes were lambent.

"Wonderful!" she enthused. "I knew you could do it." Her eyes darkened a little. "Wade," she asked, "why did you tell me?"

"Well," he smiled, "you are to a certain extent responsible for what I've accomplished."

"Yes?" she said softly. "How?"

"Because certain things you said the night Gates was here stuck in my mind—sort of gave me a little push, as it were."

"You are going to be a big man," she said slowly, but the eyes had darkened still more—was it with a trace of disappointment?

"Perhaps," he said, "and if I am, I won't forget you."

"Thank you," she said, and he noted a slight coldness in her voice that hadn't been there before. She stood up.

"Got to get back to work," she announced. "The orchestra is tuning up." She nodded as she left the table, but she did not smile.

Rawlins wondered at the abrupt change in her manner. Being a man, he could not be expected to understand.

Seven

The bonanza times continued. Everybody had money. Everybody was filled with optimism and expectations of riches to come.

The oil was moving now. Gulf schooners and side-wheel river boats nosed through Sabine Pass and up the Neches River, and plowed down again with their holds crammed and their decks stacked with barrels of the liquid treasure. At Port Arthur the cargo was transhipped to all parts of the world. The oil flowed out. Money flowed in.

But there was a cloud on the horizon, a small cloud as yet, but one which threatened to become larger and which gave the oil producers no little concern.

"It's a puzzling development and a bit ominous," Bet-a-Million Gates told Wade Rawlins in the course of one of their meetings in the Crosby House dining room. "We are constantly faced by rising shipping rates. There appears to be some sort of a combine, although none of them will admit it, of the boat captains and owners—most of the captains are owners, incidentally—and when one raises rates the others follow suit. Not all of them. There are some with whom we have contracts, and being honest men, they want to live up to their contracts."

"Any reason why they shouldn't?" Rawlins asked.

"No ethical or legal reason why they should not," Gates replied, "but they are getting worried. Seems they receive visits from men who claim to represent other captains or owners, and who, after a little persuasive talk in which they state that the oil producers are making fortunes and the shippers are getting only the leavings, hint that if they—the owners and captains—don't fall in line they may find it bad for their business or their health."

"Looks like intimidation," Rawlins commented.

"It is," Gates declared angrily, "but you'd have a devil of a time proving it. There are no threats made; just veiled hints. Oh, whoever is back of the business is shrewd, all right."

"You are of the opinion there is, shall we say, a master mind who directs the operations?"

"It's been my experience that in such a situation there is invariably an individual of power and ability who is the mainspring of it," Gates replied. "Anyhow, it looks like we're in for trouble. We can't stand much more of an increase in rates."

"I see," Rawlins replied thoughtfully. "And you are dependent on the river boats and the Gulf schooners."

"We are," Gates replied. "It's the only method of getting such quantities of oil to Port Arthur where it takes the sea."

"Which makes Port Arthur something in the nature of the key to the situation."

"Precisely," agreed Gates.

Rawlins nodded and did not pursue the discussion further, but his eyes remained thoughtful. Wade Rawlins was getting another "notion."

Rawlins liked the busy waterfront with its hurry and bustle, ships coming and going, men of all races and nationalities crowding the streets and congregating in the bars. He often strolled that way in the evening before going to work. The activities along the river stimulated thought.

One evening a couple of days after his talk with John Gates found him sauntering about on one of the wharves. He pondered the talk that was going around of a turning basin at the foot of Main and Pearl Streets, a channel twenty-five feet in depth cutting off two bends of the river and extending to the head of the Port Arthur Canal.

A big side-wheeler was just putting out from the wharf. Her stacks steaming, her paddles beating the water, she nosed slowly toward midstream. Rawlins thought she made a very beautiful picture in the red rays of the setting sun. Her decks were stacked with oil barrels and other cargo and her hold was crammed with black gold. A few figures other than seamen were moving about her upper deck; evidently she carried passengers as well as freight. Rawlins watched her idly.

She reached the middle of the river and was slowly swinging around to point her bow downstream. A few more minutes and she would be chugging along with the sluggish current.

Suddenly a shattering roar split the air, rocking the waterfront buildings, flinging back from their walls in staccato echoes. From the steamer gushed a great cloud of yellowish smoke, through which shot timbers and other woodwork and barrels of oil, some of them flaming.

"Good grief!" a voice yelled. "Her boiler busted!"

Eight

Hurled back against a stack of cargo, half stunned by the concussion, Wade Rawlins experienced a moment of bewilderment. That sharp-edged thunderous crash did not sound in the least like the sullen boom of an exploding boiler, something he had once heard on the Mississippi.

"That was dynamite or I'm a sheepherder!" he muttered, rubbing a bruised elbow. "But what in blazes was dynamite doing on an oil ship!"

In a matter of seconds the steamer was a seething inferno, spouting smoke and fire in every direction; screams of pain and terror sounded.

Tense with horror, Rawlins rushed to the wharf edge and stood staring through the smoke clouds. He could see figures climbing over the rail and dropping to the water, risking broken necks, drowning, anything to escape the raging furnace at their backs.

But now a new horror was added to a situation already horrible enough. The water was covered with oil from the shattered barrels, and the floating oil had caught fire. Flickering flames spread over the surface of the river, glaring up at the blazing ship that had swung broadside to the current. Now the gasses from the heated oil were exploding; the flaming drums skyrocketed through the air to add their rain of fiery drops to the conflagration raging on the water. Shrieks of agony rose from the doomed wretches caught in the flaming downpour. The shoreline was a pandemonium of shouts, yells and curses from the swelling crowd that stood helpless in the face of disaster.

Directly out from where Rawlins stood, a score or so yards from the wharf, was a crescent of burning oil that swept slowly around in a shallow curve which would soon form a complete circle. And in the middle of the narrowing curve was a struggling figure. Rawlins strained forward to better see the white face outlined in the glare of the fire. He gulped.

The face was the face of a woman!

For an instant Rawlins stood numb, staring at the girl's agonized face. Then he whipped off his long coat and dropped it to the ground, casting his hat aside in the same gesture. He unbuckled his gun belts and thrust the heavy Colts at a man standing rigid beside him.

"Hold them!" he said, and dived into the river.

Wade Rawlins was a fast swimmer but, encumbered by his clothes, his pace seemed an agonized snail-crawl as he fought to reach the struggling girl before the slowly rolling crescent of fire closed about her in a deadly circle. His jaws clamped tight as he swam through the narrow channel of clear water that still lay between the closing horns of burning oil. There was no turning back now; it was safety or a fiery death. He stroked with all his strength. The burning oil rolled on.

He could see her face plainly now. It was as white as a flower in the glare of the flames, and her eyes were great dark pools of terror; but she showed no signs of panic and kept paddling grimly.

"Don't grab hold of me," he shouted as he drew near. She did not cry out; merely ducked her head in a nod of understanding. Rawlins reached her and twisted his body around.

"Put your hands on my shoulders," he gasped. "Don't clutch, but hold on tight. Let your body trail. Steady now—that's right. Here we go!"

A cold thrill shot through him as he glanced at the narrowing ring of fire. There wasn't a chance in a hundred of getting through the closing channel of clear water before the circle was complete. The steamer, low in the water from the river pouring through the rents in her shattered hull, had caught on a snag or a bar and hung broadside to the current; oil from the burst barrels spurted over the surface of the stream to feed the roaring flames. But with grim determination he struck out for the shore where men danced and yelled in consternation.

Strong swimmer though he was, Rawlins was

beginning to weaken. The drag of the girl's weight and the downward pull of his drenched clothes drained away his strength, and the water was cold, its icy bite eating into his bones, numbing his muscles. Queer flickers of orange and red that were not from the flames sped back and forth before his eyes. There was an iron band around his chest, tightening, tightening. And the fiery horns of the crescent, caught in an eddy, swirled ever closer. Now they were roaring on either side but a few yards distant. Rawlins shot another glance at them and half turned his head.

"Duck your face under the water and hold it there as long as you can," he croaked to the girl. "And for Pete's sake don't lose your hold!"

He put forth the last remnant of his failing strength. He was between the closing horns. Their furnace breath seared his face. He felt his eyelashes crisp. His lung swelled, but there was no air to breathe; only reeking, fiery fumes that scorched his throat and set his senses to whirling. He beat the water madly with his arms. A tongue of flame curled over one hand and wrist. The sharp agony of it jolted him back from the black reek of unconsciousness into which he was sinking. He made a last supreme effort, surging forward through the flame-streaked water.

Suddenly before his eyes was darkness, or what seemed to him darkness after the dazzling blaze of the fire. It took him a moment to understand; they were through! Ahead, less than a score of feet distant, was the wharf and hands that reached down to him. A few more exhausted strokes and one of the hands clutched his wrist. He was hauled to safety, the girl still clinging to him like a limpet to a stone.

For several moments Rawlins lay supine on the rough planks, utterly exhausted, his breath coming in great gulps. Then he managed to struggle to a sitting position. Ready hands helped him to rise and supported him till he was steady on his feet.

"Here's your guns, feller," a voice said. "I held 'em!"

Rawlins muttered a word of thanks and buckled on the Colts. Another well-wisher, inarticulate with excitement, was desperately endeavoring to force him into his coat, wrong side first. He succeeded in reversing the garment and drew it about him gratefully, for his teeth were chattering with cold although the air was comparatively warm. Somebody else brought his hat.

A man came running with a can of grease. "Here, feller, let me daub this on your face and hands," he said. "It won't look purty, but it'll keep you from blistering; you're scorched."

The grease felt cool and soothing to his smarting face and Rawlins did not resist the other's ministrations. His benefactor stepped back with a chuckle.

"Just like an end man in a minstrel show," he said, "but it'll make you feel a lot better tomorrow."

Others had been looking after the girl, who was also on her feet. Rawlins noted that her wet hair was the color of ripe corn silk and that her eyes, in startling contrast to the hair and her blonde coloring, were black.

"We've got to get you into some dry clothes," he told her. "Don't want you to get a chill. Where—"

"To the Crosby House," she interrupted. "My father has rooms there. I was going to Port Arthur for a few days with him. I'm Marion Loche."

The name had a familiar ring. Abruptly Rawlins recalled where he had heard it. Jules Loche, said to be of New England birth, was a shrewd and resourceful promoter who had arrived at Beaumont not long before the oil strike. He had realized what a strike would do to the sagging lumber business and had gambled on Spindletop coming in. Before the first gusher roared out of the ground, he had bought several mills at a ridiculously low figure. When they were worth five or six times what he paid for them, he sold out and with the money purchased a big block of stock in the ramshackle railroad Arthur Stillwell built for the sole purpose of freighting supplies from Beaumont to his booming new port town. Now the railroad also carried oil, all it could handle. It was only a small portion of the production but enough to cause the stock to soar. Rawlins believed Loche would soon sell out again and wondered what he'd turn his hand to next. However, he merely nodded and supplied his own name.

The doomed steamer was still burning fiercely, and the whole river surface was a mass of flame. Men were wetting down the docks and the walls of nearby buildings, and other shipping was getting away from there as fast as it could.

"Everybody get ashore safe?" Rawlins asked a man as they started across the wharf.

"We pulled out a lot of folks, but I'm scared some got burned up or killed by the explosion," the other replied. "Guess if it hadn't been for you, feller, there'd have been one more," he added with a meaningful glance at Marion Loche. He hurried off to fill a bucket with water. Rawlins and his companion continued on their way. The girl glanced up at him with a wan smile.

"If there was a laugh left in me, I'd really have to laugh, even though you saved my life," she said. "You look so funny with all that black grease on your face."

Rawlins didn't know whether to be offended or amused. He compromised by saying, "Hurry up, and walk as fast as you can; you're shivering."

When they reached the Crosby House, which wasn't far off, they found the place deserted save for the desk clerk and a couple of bellhops; everybody else had hurried to the scene of the disaster.

The clerk came from behind his desk to greet them. "Miss Loche, I'm so glad to see you safe!" he exclaimed. "We were afraid—"

"And that's just what would have happened if it hadn't been for Mr. Rawlins here," the girl replied. "Give me my key, please. I must get these wet things off. I'm freezing."

"I'll call one of the maids to help you," the clerk volunteered as he passed her the key.

Rawlins accompanied her to the door of her room on the second floor. At the door she held out a slender hand.

"I'm not going to try to thank you for what you did," she said. "At such a time words are inadequate. Now hurry and get into dry clothes yourself. Then you'll come to see me?"

"I have to work tonight, but I'll try to drop around tomorrow if I may," he replied.

"I'll be expecting you," she said. She glanced over her shoulder before she closed the door, an inscrutable expression in her black eyes, and a spot of color burned in each creamily tanned cheek. She closed the door slowly.

Leaving the hotel, Rawlins headed for his own room and a change of clothing. Clean and decent once more, he sat down and smoked a cigarette before repairing to the Alhambra. He was already late but suspected that there would be very little business going on.

In fact, when he arrived at the saloon, only Crane Francis and the help were there. Francis shot him a curious glance.

"You down at the dock?" he asked. Rawlins nodded.

"Just what did happen?" Francis asked. "We heard the blast; then a fellow ran in and yelled that one of the boats had blown up. Everybody hightailed and nobody's been back since. Did a boiler explode?"

"That's what I heard somebody say they figured it was," Rawlins replied. He did not care to discuss his own opinion of what had happened, because of an unpleasant suspicion that had crawled into his mind.

"What happened to you—why are you greased up?" Francis asked.

"I got a bit too close to the fire," Rawlins drawled.

Francis favored him with another curious look but asked no more questions about the matter, apparently sensing that they would not be answered. He broached a safer subject:

"Ship a total loss?"

"Looked that way to me," Rawlins answered. "She'd burned down to the hull when I left."

Having nothing else to do, Rawlins occupied a table and ordered something to eat. Soon, however, the saloon began to fill up and he was immediately the recipient of admiring glances and congratulations.

"Darned if it wasn't the bravest thing I ever saw," one enthusiast declared in a voice that carried to all parts of the room. "He jumped right into that blazin' fire and pulled her out. We figured they were both goners for a while, but he made it, with the burnin' oil rolling all over him. The girl sure would have been one if it wasn't for him."

There was much more of a similar nature, and Wade heartily wished he were elsewhere.

When Audrey joined him as he was having his after-midnight snack, she did not hesitate to bring up the subject.

"So it was a lady this time," she observed, dropping into a chair and smoothing her short skirt over her rounded knees. "Always *le parfait* knight, *sans peur et sans reproche.*"

"Where did you learn to speak French?" he asked wonderingly.

"At Miss Lucretia Sadler's Finishing School for Young Ladies, in Boston," she answered, deliciously imitating the New England twang as she chanted the pompous title.

Rawlins stared at her. "Audrey, what the devil *are* you doing in this place?" he demanded.

"As I told you once before, earning an honest living."

Rawlins snorted his exasperation. "I can't make you out," he complained.

"What man can ever make a woman out?" she retorted. "Be thankful that you can't, and remain happy in your ignorance."

"Now what do you mean by that?" he asked.

"I mean that if a man ever succeeded in rightly reading a woman's mind, he'd be so bewildered he'd have no peace for the rest of his days."

"You may have something there," he conceded. "Take 'em as you find 'em."

"As and when," she said. "Is she pretty? I mean the damsel you dared the dragon's fiery jaws to rescue."

"Why, I guess she'll pass," he answered, slightly taken aback by the sudden shift. "She looked like a drowned kitten. I noticed she has yellow hair and black eyes, an odd combination."

"Happens sometimes," Audrey said. "Did you learn who she is?"

"Yes, Jules Loche's daughter," he replied. Audrey's big eyes widened a trifle and there was a peculiar expression in their blue depths.

"You may have heard of him," Rawlins continued. "He's pretty well known in Beaumont and Port Arthur."

"Yes, I've heard of him," she said slowly. "I

understand he's something of a character, and as full of surprises as yourself."

"I've gathered that he's a shrewd promoter," Rawlins said. "I know nothing of him as a person."

"I imagine you're destined to know more," Audrey predicted. "That is, if he has any gratitude in him. He could hardly refrain from seeking you out."

"I'd rather he didn't," Rawlins growled. "After all, I didn't do anything any other man wouldn't have, under the circumstances."

"It would appear nobody else even attempted to do it," she reminded him pointedly.

"I just happened to be there first," Rawlins answered with a smile.

"And got out without help from anyone," she commented dryly. "Well, there goes the music. Be seeing you."

She sauntered back to the dance floor. Rawlins watched her go and shook his head. He liked her, but she was too much of an enigma to be a comfortable companion.

Nine

Rawlins was awakened about noon the next day by a persistent knocking. He opened the door to admit a messenger from the Crosby House who handed him a sealed envelope. He tore it open and read:

> Would like to see you this afternoon. Drop around if you have the time.
>
> (signed) Gates

Recalling that he had another tentative appointment at the Crosby House, Wade Rawlins shaved and dressed with care. He was honest enough with himself to admit that he hankered to show Marion Loche that he did not normally resemble an end man in a minstrel show. His face was tender and somewhat reddened, but the swift application of the grease had prevented his deeply bronzed skin from blistering. After a leisurely breakfast he headed for the hotel.

Gates was not in the lobby when he arrived, but the head waiter, who evidently had his orders, met him at once and conducted him not to the dining room but to the financier's rooms upstairs. There he found Gates, former Governor

Hogg, Jim Swayne and several other gentlemen he didn't know seated around a table—all looked very serious.

Gates performed the introductions and waved him to a chair.

"Wade," he said, "I believe you were down on the wharf when the explosion occurred yesterday evening?" Rawlins nodded.

"Did it sound to you like the boiler let go?"

"It did not," Rawlins stated positively. "That was not an exploding boiler; it was dynamite. I've handled too much of the stuff not to know. But what was dynamite doing on an oil boat?"

"That's what we'd like to know," Gates answered grimly. Rawlins stared at him in silence for a moment.

"So you believe the stuff was planted and deliberately set off?" he asked.

"Well, that boat was owned by a skipper who received a veiled threat after he refused to join the combine," said Gates. "Be that as it may, the boat is a total loss and six persons died. I gather that had it not been for your courage and ability, the number would be seven."

"Possibly," Rawlins conceded. "So it would seem that somebody is willing to do murder to achieve his ends."

"Murder was done," Gates said. "We are all convinced that the boat was deliberately destroyed to throw fear into the other independent owners. We wanted to know what you thought; that's why we sent for you when we learned you were there."

"I'll repeat, I'm positive it was a dynamite explosion and not a bursting boiler," Rawlins said.

"And we're just as positive that you are right," Gates said. "The trouble is we can't prove anything. All sorts of rumors are flying around, but yours is about the only authentic statement we've been able to tie onto."

"What does the skipper think?" Rawlins asked.

"He's not doing anything, at least not in this world," Gates answered shortly.

"Killed, eh?"

"Yes, and so were two of the three men in the engine room at the time. The third was too dazed to be able to say for sure whether the boiler exploded or not. Appears the charge was set in or near the engine room."

Rawlins nodded, his pale eyes cold. His suspicion of the night before had been sound.

"One thing is certain: we're in for trouble," remarked Jim Hogg.

"You can say that double," growled Swayne. "A little more of this and they'll have us where the hair is short and we'll have to knuckle under to their demands."

"The question is: what's to be done about it?" observed Wade Rawlins.

"A hard question to answer," grunted Bet-a-Million Gates.

Wade Rawlins swept a glance over the gloomy gathering. He was convinced opportunity had knocked again.

"Gentlemen," he said slowly, "I believe I have the answer. I'm not prepared to speak what is in my mind at the moment, but if you'll give me a little time, I'm pretty certain I can provide the answer."

All eyes were turned on the speaker.

It was Bet-a-Million Gates who broke the silence. "Well, son," he said, "I've seen you in action and I'm inclined to string along with whatever you have in mind. I hope it's good, for nobody else seems able to think of anything. So go to it."

The others nodded sober agreement.

"Will it take long?" asked Swayne.

"Just a few days," Rawlins replied. "I'll get busy right away," he added, rising to his feet. With a nod he left the room.

Jules Loche's rooms were on the floor above. Rawlins hesitated at the door, then knocked. There was a sound of somebody moving about inside, and the door opened to reveal Marion Loche, a look of polite inquiry on her face, which quickly was replaced by a radiant smile.

"Come in!" she exclaimed. "I didn't recognize you at first. You look different."

"Less like the end man of a minstrel show?" he replied, entering and tossing his hat aside.

"I never thought you looked like that," she protested. "With the black grease making a mustache and a short beard, you reminded me of a picture I once saw of the Spanish guerrilla leader, Mina."

"Or some other brigand?" he smiled.

"Was he a brigand? I gathered that he was a general and a patriot. But never mind; anyhow, he was very striking-looking. Sit down while I get us a drink. Oh, yes, I drink and smoke, too. Are you properly shocked?"

"Nothing wrong about drinking or smoking, if they're done gracefully," he replied, "and in your case they must be."

"Thank you, sir," she said demurely. "I hope you won't be disillusioned."

She crossed the room with lithe grace and passed through an inner door. Rawlins decided she didn't look at all like a drowned kitten now; she looked lovely, with her yellow hair done in curls that clustered about the delicate oval of her small face, and her flashing black eyes.

The tastefully furnished big and airy room had a distinctly feminine touch. There were paints and prints on the walls that certainly had not been hung there by the management of the Crosby House. The same went, he felt pretty certain, for the other pieces scattered about.

"I fixed it up myself," she said, interpreting his

glance as she returned with two tall glasses, one of which she handed to him. "I had the original furnishings moved out and replaced them with others more to my liking. I spend a lot of time in hotels, with Dad moving about as he always is, and I like to try and make a place home-like."

"You certainly succeeded here," he commented.

"I'm glad you like it," she said. She sat down opposite him, crossed her knees and regarded him over the rim of her glass.

"Just what do you do for a living, Mr. Rawlins, if I'm not impertinent in asking?" she said.

"I deal cards at the Alhambra Saloon," he replied.

She nodded. "Among other things, I imagine. I've never been there."

"Ask your father to take you in sometime; we have feminine patronage, now and then."

"I will," she answered, "although Dad doesn't visit saloons much; he prefers to do his drinking at home. That's how I came to acquire the habit."

"Your complexion attests to the fact that you've not acquired it seriously," he returned.

She laughed and produced a package of cigarettes, offering it to him.

"I prefer to roll my own," he declined. "A cowhand is never much on tailor-mades. Here's a light for yours."

"So you're a cowhand, too?" she commented.

"I don't know much about cowboys, but I've always understood they are very dashing and romantic figures."

Rawlins chuckled, calling to mind various specimens with whom he had worked.

"A cowboy is just a hired man on horseback," he pointed out.

"I think a horse makes any man look dashing and romantic," she said. "Certainly more so than our rapidly developing new means of transportation, the automobile."

"I imagine a romantic figure is a romantic figure no matter what the setting," he answered. "And you'd better get used to regarding the automobile as a romantic conveyance. Very soon it will largely displace the horse."

"Which will be good for the oil business, will it not?" she asked.

"It certainly will," he replied, and wondered what prompted the question.

She did not pursue the subject and regarded him over the rim of her glass for a moment of silence.

"Mr. Rawlins," she said suddenly, "do all card dealers and cowhands speak as you do?"

"Well, not all," he admitted with a smile. "I am one of the more fortunate ones; I managed to get a little education before my father died."

"And I managed to get a little before my mother died and we left Massachusetts to come west," she returned. "Not much since, of the formal variety."

"Massachusetts," he repeated. An unexplainable impulse prompted him to ask a question:

"Did you by any chance ever hear of Miss Lucretia Sadler's Finishing School for Young Ladies, in Boston?"

Her eyes widened. "Why, yes," she replied. "It is one of the most fashionable schools in New England. It is not easy to enroll in Miss Sadler's school; the requirements are rigid. Family background is necessary, among other things. And although money alone can't get you in, plenty is required. It's not a cheap school, to put it mildly. Where did you learn of it?"

"Oh, I heard somebody mention it as being in Boston," he evaded lightly, and deftly changed the subject. "You and your father did not come directly to Texas?"

"Goodness, no!" she answered. "We've lived in a great number of places—New York, Philadelphia, Chicago, St. Louis, Denver, San Francisco, among others. He is very industrious and interested in many things, such as railroads, mines, settlements, I don't know what all. Here it has been lumbering and the railroad."

"He's not interested in the oil strike, then?"

Her lashes, very long and thick lashes, he noted, lowered for a moment, as in thought.

"I really don't know," she replied. "He has

seemed to concern himself chiefly with the byproducts of the oil strike."

Rawlins nodded.

"You'll come again soon, won't you?" she said as he rose to go. "My father will be here in a few days, and he'll be as grateful for what you did as I am and will want to thank you."

"There's really no need for thanks for what was a pleasure," he answered.

"I don't think it was so pleasant at one time," she replied dryly. She shuddered. "I can still hear those flames roaring," she said. "But please come again—soon."

Wade Rawlins left the Crosby House in a troubled mood; he didn't know just what to make of Marion Loche.

He tried to put her out of his mind, for he had plenty of other things that required serious thought, but she kept intruding. He swore querulously and headed for the Alhambra.

Arriving at the saloon, he at once approached Francis. "Well, Crane, I'm leaving you," he announced.

Francis did not look surprised. "Figured you wouldn't stay much longer after you got to hobnobbing with Gates and his crowd," he said. "Well, they can pay you better than I can afford to, and after all, there isn't much of a future in dealing cards. Going to work tonight?"

"Yes, I'll stay on tonight," Rawlins replied.

"I've been coaching Pete, and I feel he can handle the chore in a satisfactory manner."

"Pete's all right," agreed Francis. "Good luck to you."

His smile was peculiar, and there was a mocking light in his alert eyes as he turned away.

Rawlins had something to eat and then spoke with Audrey, who had come onto the floor.

"I'm glad you're striking out for yourself, but I'll miss you," she said.

"Don't worry; I'll be dropping in regularly," he promised. "And if things don't work out right, I'm liable to be coming back looking for a job," he added with a grin.

"Oh, no, you won't!" she predicted. "You'll end up a big man, Wade."

"Maybe," he conceded moodily. "After all, what is a big man? A man may be big in his own estimation but very small in the estimation of others."

"I fear you will have to find the answer to that for and *from* yourself," she replied. "Good luck!"

Ten

Rawlins slept till noon the following day and then rode to the Lazy V Ranch for a conference with old Roderick McArdle. He carefully outlined the plan he had in mind to the cattleman. McArdle was dubious.

"The boys have no use for the oil strike," he said. "It's caused all of us plenty of trouble; but I'll go along with you and we'll see what we can do."

The following morning he and McArdle set out, visiting the owners of ranches between Beaumont and Port Arthur. To each Rawlins broached the subject cautiously, at first with little success. As McArdle said, the owners had no use for the oil strike or anything pertaining to it. They pointed out that it had brought a host of undesirable characters into what had formerly been a peaceful section, including a number of smart, ingenious and daring cattle thieves. Since the blasted field had opened up, they had lost five times as many cows as in a similar period before. Their hands had been embroiled in ruckuses with the oil workers and the riff-raff that formed the usual camp followers of a boom. Why should they cooperate in any way with such a nuisance?

But Roderick McArdle's influence in the section was not to be lightly regarded, and Wade Rawlins was a persuasive talker. The oil strike was there and it was there to stay. They couldn't stop the wheels of progress, so wasn't it the sensible thing to make the best of conditions they couldn't alter and to take a profit from them if possible? Already, he reminded them, the boom was providing a ready market for their surplus stock at better prices than they could get elsewhere and without the expense of shipping or long drives. If they were not adverse to making money from selling beef for the consumption of the oil workers, why should they hesitate to make more money with no risk of possible loss to themselves?

There was considerable cussing and grumbling, but with each Rawlins finally won his point, and by the time he and old Roderick reached Port Arthur, his pockets were filled with signed agreements.

"Laddie, you did it!" applauded McArdle as they enjoyed a good meal in a Port Arthur saloon. "I nay ken how you did it. When we started on this traipsin', I had my doubts. You have the gift of gab."

"You didn't say much, but what you did say counted heavily," Rawlins told him. "The owners respect your opinions, and when they realized I had won you over, they were half sold already."

Old Rod chuckled and didn't argue the point.

When Wade Rawlins entered Gates' room, where the oil men were assembled, all eyes turned on him expectantly.

"Well," said Gates, "got the answer?"

"Yes, I've got the answer." Rawlins returned slowly. "Pipe lines to Port Arthur, where the oil can take the sea without any intermediary shipping."

His hearers looked grievously disappointed, as he expected them to.

"We've thought of that, of course," said Swayne. "The trouble is with the cattlemen over whose lands the lines would have to pass. They are bitter against the oil strike, and not altogether without justification. They say it has brought them a world of trouble and they don't want to have anything to do with it. There's no moving them. Sorry, Wade, but it won't work."

Wade Rawlins drew a packet of documents from his pocket.

"Gentlemen," he said, "I have here agreements signed by the owners in question, granting permission to construct the pipe lines over their lands."

A chorus of exclamations arose. Swane seized the papers like a hungry dog grabbing a bone and began to scan them with avid eyes. Suddenly a comical expression of dismay overspread his good-humored face.

"I see that you are granted the sole rights to build the lines!" he exclaimed.

"Guess that's so," Rawlins admitted.

"It's a hold-up!" wailed Swayne. "He's got us right where he wants us! Okay! Okay! I know when I'm licked. Here's my right arm to begin with. Anybody willing to put up a leg?"

Bet-a-Million Gates chuckled as he riffled through the papers.

"If I know Wade, we don't have to worry about being made to pay through the nose," he said. "He deserves a nice profit, and he'll get it. What the owners ask seems reasonable enough, too. Gentlemen, I move we render a vote of thanks to Mr. Wade Rawlins for saving what looked like an impossible situation."

The vote was given, with enthusiasm.

"You going to handle the construction of the lines?" Gates asked.

Rawlins shook his head. "I'm a halfway engineer, but I'm not an oil man," he explained. "I haven't the technical knowledge necessary to such a project. I'll run the survey lines and work out the gradients—I'm enough of an engineer for that—but that's as far as I care to trust myself. The actual construction is beyond me. However, I know a man who has the necessary knowledge and ability, and I believe we can persuade him to take over the chore."

"Who is it?" asked Hogg.

"Jason Abbot, who optioned me his oil," Rawlins replied. "He has nearly a dozen producing wells, but this sort of a chore would appeal to him. He's by nature a wildcatter, just like Tony Lucas who brought in the first Spindletop gusher. Abbot would get more satisfaction from opening up a new field than from the money his producing wells make for him. He's in for anything that's a bit different, and of course he'll profit from the pipe lines, too."

"I remember him; I liked him," said Gates. "Try and get him here tomorrow and we'll have a talk. But I think you should superintend the job, Wade, on a salary basis."

"I'd like to do that," Rawlins agreed. "We may run up against difficulties. The combine, if there is such a thing, isn't going to like it and may figure a way to make trouble."

Three days later the earth was gashed for the first pipe line in southeast Texas.

The start of the project was something of an event. All the big men of the local oil field were present. Bet-a-Million Gates insisted that Rawlins turn the first spadeful of earth, which he did to the accompaniment of cheers. Then Jason Abbot took over, swearing strange oaths and telling his grinning workers what would happen to them if they loafed on the job.

There was no loafing; Abbot was too popular with his man for them to let him down in any way. They worked with a will and appeared to enjoy the attention they attracted, on the job and in the Alhambra saloons. Somebody named them Abbot's Gophers; they didn't resent it.

And it wasn't long before they extended their respect and liking to Wade Rawlins.

Abbot's pressing problem was labor, or rather, the lack of it. The installation of the pumping machinery and the laying of the line required skilled mechanics with special training, and there were all too few of them available.

"I sent a hurry-up call east for pipe fitters in particular," he told Rawlins. "But it's hard to get competent men to come out here, even with high wages and a bonus, on what may be a temporary basis."

"It probably won't be so temporary," Rawlins predicted confidently. "This won't be the only line laid, or anything like it; with production increasing all the time, it will require a number of lines to handle the output."

"I think you're right," Abbot agreed. "Well, we'll do the best we can with what we've got till some more roll in."

"We'll also need companion 'products' lines for gasoline and light fuel oils as soon as the refineries get going strong," Rawlins observed. "It's a big project, Jason, and will get bigger all the time."

Abbot didn't argue the point; he was willing

to take at face value anything Rawlins might say.

For several days the work went smoothly. Then, on the morning of the fourth day, trouble started.

Rawlins was setting his transit preparatory to taking a sight. One spiked tripod leg came down on a sloping stone and skidded sharply. Rawlins lunged sideways, making a grab for the sliding instrument. The transit leaped from his grasp and went end over end through the air, one leg of the tripod shattered. As he whirled about, Rawlins heard the crack of the distant rifle. His keen eyes spotted the tiny puff of smoke that drifted upward from the edge of a small thicket nearly six hundred yards distant.

"Down!" he yelled to his helpers. "Hunt cover!" As he raced toward where Flame stood, ears pricked forward inquiringly, a second slug fanned his face with its lethal breath. Reaching the horse, he jerked his heavy Winchester from the saddle boot and dropped to one knee.

Back and forth, he sprayed the distant thicket with a stream of lead. The ejecting lever of the rifle was a blur of movement; had a cartridge jammed, the tough steel would have shattered like matchwood.

There were still two cartridges in the magazine when, from the far side of the thicket, burst a horseman mounted on a tall bay, going at full speed.

Rawlins surged erect, flipped the bit into Flame's mouth and forked the sorrel in a ripple of motion.

"Trail, feller, trail!" he shouted.

With a snort Flame lunged forward. Guiding the racing horse with his knees, Rawlins stuffed fresh cartridges into the rifle's magazine, his eyes never leaving his quarry, who was speeding east across the prairie.

"If we can just run that sidewinder down and take him alive, I've a notion I can persuade him to do a little talking and maybe we'll find out who's back of this hellishness," he told the horse. "Go to it, feller; it's up to you now!"

Flame responded nobly, slugging his head above the bit, snorting and blowing with excitement and literally pouring his long body across the ground. Rawlins holstered the Winchester and gave all his attention to riding.

The big bay was giving all he had, but it wasn't enough. Slowly, steadily, Flame closed the distance. Rawlins could see the white blur of the fugitive's face as he turned to glance back at his pursuer. Far ahead gleamed the waters of the Neches rolling on to the Gulf. Apparently the drygulcher was making for the river. Rawlins estimated the distance he had to go and the lessening space that separated them.

"The devil will never make it," he told Flame exultantly. "If he takes to the water I'll wing him before he gets across. Hope he doesn't drown before I can haul him out!"

Flame seemed to understand, for he somehow managed to increase his pace a little. His eyes flashed with anger as they fixed on the insolent bay who appeared to believe he could stay ahead of a golden sorrel of pure blood.

The fleeing drygulcher was glancing back more frequently now, his head jerking nervously. Rawlins could vaguely distinguish features, the bristle of beard on his cheeks and chin, the eye sockets, with the eyes not yet clearly defined.

Closer gleamed the waters of the Neches, tossing and shining in the sun. The bay horse strained toward its glittering flood.

Suddenly the drygulcher gave up, realizing he could never make the farther shore in time. At the very edge of the bank he pulled his horse to a halt and whirled him about to face the flying sorrel. Rawlins' voice rang out:

"Steady, Flame, steady!"

Instantly the big horse leveled off in a smooth running walk. Rawlins lurched sideways as he saw the flash of the raised rifle. A spurt of smoke, and the slug yelled past. He whipped the Winchester from the boot, clamped the butt against his shoulder. A second bullet turned his hat sideways on his head. Then the Winchester gushed flame and smoke. A third bit of flying lead ripped his shirt sleeve. He jerked Flame to a halt.

Again the blur of the flashing ejection lever, the rifle muzzle weaving from side to side, belching smoke. The two duelists sat like statues, the brilliant sunshine outlining every line and feature, blasting death at each other through the crystal air.

Rawlins counted his shots as slugs buzzed past like angry hornets. Four—five—six! He steadied the rifle. Red lights blazed before his eyes as a bullet grazed his temple. Again he steadied the rifle; the devil was getting the range! If he pulled trigger again—

At the seventh shot the drygulcher reeled. He clutched at the saddle horn, dropped his rifle, then slid from the hull like a wounded bird from its perch. He slid quite slowly, as if utterly weary and seeking rest. His body bounced slightly as it struck the lip of the high bank, then vanished. Rawlins saw the glitter of the drops of spray; he did not hear the splash. He slammed the Winchester back in the boot.

"Trail, Flame, trail!" The sorrel shot forward. But when the blowing horse pulled up at the edge of the bank, only the dark Neches was to be seen, gleaming mockingly in the sun. Somewhere far to the south a lifeless thing hurried on toward its last resting place in the blue waters of the Gulf.

Raising a hand that shook a little, Rawlins wiped the sweat from his face, along with a trickle of blood from his bullet-burned temple.

He stared at the dark river and his lips moved.

"Five!" he muttered. "I'm beginning to wish I'd stayed in New Orleans!"

Turning Flame, he rode slowly back the way he had come, his usually erect figure slumping in the saddle, his eyes staring straight ahead.

Eleven

When Rawlins got back to the survey line he found his helpers squatting comfortably on the prairie, smoking.

"Get him?" the rod man asked.

"He went into the Neches," Rawlins replied. "Well, let's see if we can patch up that tripod and get back to work."

The others nodded and asked no more questions, realizing he was in no mood to discuss the matter. The tripod was put together, after a fashion. Rawlins decided it would do until they got back to Beaumont. The rod man's check of the sighted figures resumed, and the cheerful "Stick!" "Stuck!" of the chain men, punctuated by the thud of sledge hammers on the stakes.

When it came time to knock off work, Rawlins called his helpers together for a conference.

"What happened today may be just the beginning," he told them. "Today everybody was lucky, especially myself. If I hadn't made a grab for that tumbling tripod just as the hellion pulled trigger, it might have been me instead of the tripod leg which stopped the slug. Next time somebody else may be the target, so I'm putting it up to you fellows squarely: I'm not asking anybody to take such chances. If you care to stay on the job, fine! If you prefer not to, that's okay by me and I won't think any the worse of you. You're not paid to risk your lives—this is supposed to be a chore without occupational hazards. So it's strictly up to you."

There was a moment of silence; then the rod man, a leathery-faced individual past middle age, spoke up.

"Son," he said, "I've packed a rod and handled a chain all over the world, sometimes in countries where if they don't like you they show it by roasting you over a slow fire or slicing you up, slow and easy-like, with small knives. So I don't figure to be buffaloed by flying lead. Tomorrow I'll be heeled proper, and if the sneaking, yellow-blacked sons come looking for trouble we'll give it to 'em till it runs out of their ears. And I think that goes for the rest of the boys."

A general nodding of heads corroborated his surmise.

"Okay, and thanks a lot," Rawlins said. "You're men to ride the river with; I won't forget it. Now let's head for town and something to eat and a couple of rounds of drinks—my treat."

The chain and stake men, brawny young fellows with reckless eyes, raised a cheer. "Hurrah for the Old Man!" they shouted.

As they mounted their horses, the old rod man

reined in close to Rawlins, who was riding a bit to the rear.

"Son, you're accepted, and for good and all," he chuckled. "You might be sixty 'stead of on the sunny side of thirty, and those devils wouldn't call you the 'Old Man' if they didn't figure you to be a boss worth working for and sticking by. You'll be the Old Man to them and the rest of the construction gang from now on."

Wade Rawlins nodded and smiled, and wondered whimsically if the respect shown to Bet-a-Million Gates, Jim Hogg, and Swayne by their fellows, the respect he craved, was really a higher accolade.

Rawlins cared for his horse, washed up and joined the others in the Alhambra. An excellent dinner was consumed with gusto and drinks ordered. They were working on the second round when a messenger from the Crosby House entered, spotted Rawlins and handed him a sealed envelope. His name was written on the front in a hand that was distinctly feminine. With a murmured word of apology to his companions he opened it and read:

Dear Wade,
    Please drop in on us tonight. My father is here and wishes to see you.
                              Your friend,
                              Marion

Rawlins read the note twice, folded it and stuffed it into his pocket, and ordered another round of drinks. While his companions chatted together he sat silent, pondering what he should do. He finished his drink and stood up.

"See you in the morning, boys," he said. He beckoned a waiter, ordered still another round and left the saloon.

Marion Loche herself opened the door to his knock. "Dad," she called over her shoulder, "here he is—the gentleman to whom you owe a daughter. Come in, Wade; Dad wishes to express his appreciation to you for hauling me out of the river."

Jules Loche was a big tawny-haired man with keen eyes, a prominent nose and a thin-lipped, tight mouth. His smile was cordial, however, and he shook hands heartily.

"No use for me even to try to express my appreciation, Mr. Rawlins," he said. "If you ever get married and have a daughter of your own, then you'll understand how I feel. Sit down, please. Marion, mix us a drink."

Over the rim of his glass, Jules Loche regarded Rawlins. "Understand you're making something of a splash in local financial circles," he observed.

"A very small one, I fear," Rawlins smilingly deprecated.

"Anybody who gets the jump on Jim Hogg

and his crowd makes more than a ripple," Loche differed. "Securing those pipe line options was a master stroke on your part. Hogg and Swayne are still mumbling about it under their whiskers and wondering how you did it; they'd have been willing to swear it couldn't be done."

"Guess I was just lucky," Rawlins answered.

"Perhaps, but I'd have another name for it," Loche said dryly. "Anyhow, you are to be congratulated. Also, you appear to have made a firm friend of old Bet-a-Million Gates, and that's a feat few have been able to perform. Gates is the lone wolf type and seldom becomes intimate with anybody. Business first is usually Gates' motto, and he seldom allows sentiment to influence him. I suppose you plan to stay with the Hogg-Swayne Syndicate?"

"I have had no offers from them beyond the pipe line job," Rawlins equivocated.

"Might be a good notion to go on your own, though, don't you think?" Loche prodded casually.

"There would be advantages in tying up with the Syndicate," Rawlins replied evasively.

Loche's eyes narrowed the merest trifle and his mouth tightened a little; Rawlins thought there was a slightly baffled expression in his eyes, and wondered why.

"Marion, mix us a drink," Loche said.

Loche finished his glass first. He stood up abruptly and reached for his hat.

"You young people can stay here and enjoy yourselves," he said. "I've got to go down to the lobby and try and wrangle an honest dollar. Again I thank you for what you did, Mr. Rawlins— not adequately, for that is impossible, but sincerely."

With a flourish of his hat he walked to the door, opened it and departed.

"Well, that's that," Marion said with a resigned sigh. "I hate business talks; I know nothing about it and have to sit silent like a bump on a log."

"But you are very ornamental." Rawlins smiled.

Miss Loche's rejoinder was an undignified sniff. "When two men get to talking business, a woman just doesn't exist, and you know it," she said. "You never even looked in my direction while Dad was talking."

"Sometimes one makes a supreme sacrifice in deference to courtesy," he returned.

Marion laughed. "That was nicely said, at least," she remarked. "And you have decided to be a lone wolf and go it on your own?"

"It would be rash for me to predict my future moves," he answered. "I fear they will be dependent on the development of events."

"And do you not plan and build for the future, a glorious future?"

"Sufficient unto eternity is the glory of the hour."

Her eyes lifted to meet his, an inscrutable expression in their dark depths.

"The hour," she repeated.

"It is all we have."

It was not very late when Wade left, and he decided to drop in at the Alhambra for a few minutes. He occupied a vacant table near the dance floor and ordered a drink. During an intermission, Audrey came over and sat down opposite him. And for the second time that night he was the recipient of a feminine sniff.

"You smell of perfume," she said.

"Well, I certainly don't use it," he declared.

"Of course not, but *she* does."

"She?"

"Of course, the damsel that you rescued from distress. Well, she has good taste, at least in perfume."

"And she doesn't level shafts barbed with sarcasm at me," he retorted.

" 'The guilty flee when no man pursueth.' "

"Guilty of what?"

"Whatever it is that causes you to rise so quickly to the lady's defense."

"I'm not rising to her defense; I'm merely trying to defend myself against your claws. You're in a mood tonight!"

"I'm sorry," she said. "Perhaps I'm just a little tired; it's been a trying night."

The big eyes were slightly wistful, and he was

instantly contrite; she had more than once proven herself a true friend.

"I should think you could find something easier to do than this," he said.

"Perhaps," she admitted, "but it would lack the opportunities this job provides."

Abruptly he experienced an unreasonable anger.

"I don't like the way you said that!" he exclaimed.

Her eyes met his and he reflected that they were exactly the same color as Texas bluebells under a golden sun.

"Why?" she asked.

"I don't know," he floundered, "but I don't."

The shadow of a smile drifted across the blue eyes, but she did not speak.

Rawlins felt he was getting more and more out of his depth all the time; he changed the subject.

"Where's Francis?" he asked. "Don't see him around."

"A man came in and spoke to him about an hour ago," she replied. "He grabbed his hat and hurried out. He's been doing that quite frequently of late. Well, there goes the music; got to get back to work."

She swayed gracefully back to the dance floor and a moment later she was laughing up into the face of a gay young cowhand who showed plainly that he was more than slightly satisfied with his partner. Rawlins watched them moodily for a few minutes, then left the saloon and headed for bed.

Twelve

When Rawlins arrived at the scene of operations on the pipe line the following morning, he found Jason Abbot in anything but a good temper.

"Three of my best men!" the oil man stormed. "They got into a row with some toughs in a Beaumont saloon last night. Result, one with a broken arm, another with a dislocated hip and the third with his head split open. He may be back on the job within a few days, but the Lord only knows when the other two will be able to work, and me short-handed as it was."

"How did it happen?" Rawlins asked.

"They said they were sitting at a table drinking and minding their own business, and that half a dozen hellions jumped them for no good reason at all," Abbot replied. "Didn't use guns or knives, just fists and feet and clubs, but gave them a thorough going over before the floor men and the bartenders could bust it up. I take that yarn with quite a few grains of salt; been my experience that fights don't cut loose without a reason."

"Yes, they seldom start without a reason, but sometimes the reason is not apparent," Rawlins remarked thoughtfully.

"What do you mean by that?" Abbot asked.

115

"I don't know for sure just yet," Rawlins answered. "Where do your men usually do their drinking?"

"At the Ace-Full on Pine Street, where the row busted out last night, and at the Crystal Bar, a few doors farther down the street."

"The Ace-Full and the Crystal Bar," Rawlins repeated. "Well, so long; I'll get my bunch together and head for the survey line. Wouldn't be surprised if we camp out tomorrow night; getting quite a way from town now."

The surveyors were very much on the alert, but the day passed without untoward incident. By evening, Rawlins estimated they had covered something more than half the twenty-odd miles they would have to negotiate to reach Port Arthur. So far they had encountered no very difficult obstacles.

As he rode into Beaumont through the lovely blue dusk, Wade Rawlins would have been surprised, to put it mildly, could he have known the identity of the visitor Jules Roche was entertaining at the moment. Crane Francis, handsome, debonair, lounged in the chair he himself had occupied the night before, while Marion mixed drinks for him and her father. And the subject under discussion was Wade Rawlins.

"I couldn't get anything out of him, and neither could Marion," Loche was declaring angrily. "He talked, but he didn't say anything. There's no

116

doubt but that he's got something up his sleeve, and I'm willing to wager that whatever the devil it is, it's big. Anyhow, we've got to slow up that infernal pipe line, and either learn what Rawlins has in mind or, as you say, get rid of him."

"Haven't had much luck getting rid of him so far," Francis commented dryly. "Everybody who tries it just naturally shows up among the missing. Nobody has been able to figure what became of little Pete. Westmacote went into the river, according to what Rawlins said, and he wouldn't say anything else. In my opinion, Westmacote wasn't overly lively when he hit the water."

"He's a nuisance," growled Loche, "and he's been upsetting our applecart right along. There isn't much doubt, either, but that he's the front man for Gates and Hogg and their crowd."

"Front man, nothing!" scoffed Francis. "That big devil isn't a front man for anybody and never will be. He's on his own, which makes him doubly dangerous. Yes, something's got to be done about him one way or the other; perhaps his luck won't hold forever."

"We'll get him sooner or later," said Loche.

"There's one thing you both seem to overlook when you speak of getting rid of him," Marion said slowly.

"What's that?" grunted her father.

"That he saved my life, at the risk of his own."

Jules Loche looked uncomfortable, but Crane Francis only smiled a thin, impersonal smile that never reached his fine dark eyes.

"Nobody doubts his courage," he remarked. "He'd charge hell with a bucket of water. And I'm willing to admit that he did us all a great favor when he hauled you out of the river, and he did me a personal favor when he downed that pair of skunks who tried to rob my safe; but what we are working for is too big for us to let sentiment be a factor."

"That's right," nodded Loche.

Marion said nothing more, but there was a sullen look in her eyes. The look softened, however, as they rested on Crane Francis' classically molded features, and she drew a deep breath.

Rawlins ate his dinner at the Alhambra, after which he returned to his room and for a long time sat by the open window, smoking and thinking. The hour was nearing midnight when he arose and donned a garment he had not worn for some time, his long black coat with the sleeve holster, in which rested the stubby double-barreled derringer, the "gambler's gun." Making sure his big Colts were in perfect working order, he left the hotel sauntered along Main Street to where it joined Pine Street not far from Long Avenue. He slowed his pace, glancing into the various saloons that lined the street. He passed the Ace-Full, reasoning that trouble was not apt to hit there two nights hand-running, and continued until he passed before the plate glass of the big Crystal Bar.

The place was crowded and busy and his unobtrusive entrance attracted no attention. He cast a quick glance around and walked along the wall, where it was shadowy, until he reached a small unoccupied table in a corner, likewise shadowy. Seating himself with his back to the wall, from where he could view the whole room, he ordered a drink and searched the crowd. Very quickly he spotted half a dozen of Abbot's pipe fitters seated at a table near the dance floor. They were drinking and trading quips with the girls on the floor and appeared to be having a good time. Rawlins dismissed them for the moment and continued to study the occupants of the saloon.

His attention centered on two tables drawn together and close to that occupied by the pipe fitters. Grouped around those tables were nearly a dozen men, hard-looking characters even for the Crystal Bar. Rawlins catalogued them as Border scum of the worst sort, the kind who would poison their own mothers if the price were right. They seemed to be taking an interest in the pipe line workers; Rawlins took a decided interest in them.

For quite a while nothing happened. The pipe fitters continued to drink and sing and chaff the dance floor girls, who answered in kind. Abruptly the heads of the group at the two tables drew together. There appeared to be a mutter of low-voiced conversation; then one of them shouted:

"Leave those girls alone, you greasy rats!"

The pipe men turned in astonishment and started to reply. The group surged to their feet and went for them.

Wade Rawlins covered the distance between him and the melee in two long bounds; he was in the thick of it before his move was noted.

Rows were common in the Crystal Bar, but not the kind of a row Wade Rawlins spearheaded that night. Chairs and tables turned to matchwoods, the girls screamed, men cursed and stormed, the bartenders uttered soothing yells that were not heeded. The walls shook at the uproar.

The "gambler's gun" has many uses, most of them lethal. Cupped in the palm of the hand, it makes a very satisfactory blackjack, and being of blued steel is considerably harder and heavier than the orthodox specimen. And Wade Rawlins knew how to apply it to the best advantage. Every time that derringer connected, blood spurted, bone crunched, and a man went down. Rawlins wasn't coming off unscathed in the pandemonium of flying fists and feet, but he gave a lot better than he took.

Back and forward reeled the battle. Bottles and glasses flew through the smoky air. Fists connected with solid thumps. The pipe fitters, outnumbered two to one, taken by surprise, were nevertheless playing their part like men; but it would have gone hard with them had it not been for Rawlins' timely intervention. His very presence gave them the encouragement they needed, and that slashing derringer was just what was needed to weight the balance in their favor.

The end came suddenly. One of the roughs, who had taken the derringer squarely in the mouth, spitting blood and curses through a hedge of splintered teeth, whipped out a gun.

Wade saw the gleam of metal. The derringer flipped forward, spat fire. The gun the rough had drawn went clattering across the floor, taking part of its owner's hand along with it. He gave a howl of pain, went scuttling through the crowd on all fours and vanished out the swinging doors.

As the second barrel of the derringer swung around to bear on them, the other devils evidently decided they'd had enough, too. They charged for the door, bowling over tables, chairs, and patrons indiscriminately, and followed their wounded companion into the night. Rawlins flipped the derringer back into his sleeve and began stanching the blood that flowed from a gashed cheek. He was in a towering rage and looked for somebody else to take it out on.

A burly florid-faced individual came shouldering his way to the front.

"Who started this, anyhow?" he demanded belligerently.

"Who are you?" Rawlins asked.

"I own this place."

"You do, eh?" Rawlins' hand shot out, grabbed him by the shirt front and shook him till his teeth rattled.

"Listen, you," he said, his voice like steel grinding on ice. "One more incident like this involving my men, and I'll bring a bunch in from the rangeland. We'll tear this place to pieces, and hang you from the only rafter left standing! Do you understand?" Another shake accented the question.

The owner, all the belligerency taken out of him, quavered that he understood.

The battered pipe fitters, none of whom had suffered serious injury, raised a cheer that set the hanging lamps to dancing:

"Hurrah for the Old Man!"

Others joined in; they didn't know what it was all about but apparently felt it was a good idea to climb on the bandwagon. Rawlins nodded his appreciation and turned to the grinning pipe men.

"Haul up another table and get back to your fun," he told them. "I'm giving you one more hour; then out of here and head for bed. We've got work to do tomorrow."

He returned to his own table, accepted the drink that an obsequious waiter brought him with the assertion that it was "on the house," explored a growing "mouse" under his left eye with sensitive fingertips, and rolled a cigarette.

At the bar a newcomer asked, "Who is that big feller, anyhow?"

"That's Wade Rawlins," an informant told him. "He's building the pipe line for the Hogg-Swayne Syndicate. He's in with Gates and Cullinan and all those big wigs, and he is one salty hombre! Gentlemen, hush!"

Wade ordered another drink, for which payment was politely but firmly refused, and settled down to wait out the hour with the pipe fitters. These, their cuts and abrasions forgotten, were being plied with drinks by a host of admirers and were generally having an uproarious time.

Indeed, they were having such a good time that Rawlins extended the hour to an hour and a half before calling on them to break it up and get going. They obeyed cheerfully and without argument.

As they were nearing the door, the bulky proprietor came hurrying across the room, bobbing and smiling and bearing in his hand a gun with one butt plate knocked off.

"The one you shot out of that hombre's hand," he said to Rawlins. "Thought you might like to have it for a souvenir."

"Thanks." Rawlins accepted it and dropped it into his coat pocket.

"You'll come again, Mr. Rawlins?" the proprietor asked anxiously.

"Sure," Rawlins promised, willing to let bygones be bygones; after all, the fellow might have had nothing to do with what had happened. "Sure, I had a good time here!"

Thirteen

The following morning, Rawlins called the workers together. "Hereafter when you are drinking in town, I want you to stick together as much as possible and always go heeled," he directed. "I don't think you have cause to fear a recurrence of what happened last night, but don't take chances."

Through Jason Abbot, he relayed similar instructions to the crew erecting the pumping station. Abbot, incidentally, was thoroughly disgruntled at not having had a chance to participate in the row of the night before.

"Why the devil didn't you take me with you?" he complained to Rawlins. "I'd enjoy getting a whack at those skunks."

"The way things are going, I wouldn't be surprised if you do get a chance, sooner or later," Rawlins predicted grimly.

The surveyors took along a mule loaded with blankets, cooking utensils and provisions, for Rawlins decided to camp out one night and afterward, in the evenings, to ride on to Port Arthur to sleep until the chore was finished.

Good progress was made during the day; nothing out of the way happened. That night they pitched camp on the bank of a little stream and ate their simple meal under the stars. The men were for spreading their blankets beside the campfire, but Rawlins quickly vetoed that.

"Oh, no, you don't, not after what happened the other day," he told them. "We sleep over by those bushes, in the shadow, not beside a lighted campfire where we'd be settin' quail for any sneaking drygulcher with notions."

Rawlins had no way of knowing if his precaution was really necessary, but anyhow their sleep was not interrupted, and early morning found them on their way. That evening they rode to Port Arthur, now less than ten miles distant, to spend the night in the booming shipping center situated on the west shore of Lake Sabine and about fifteen miles from the Gulf of Mexico.

Another day and a half and the survey line was complete. Rawlins and his helpers celebrated with a good dinner and a few drinks. Then Rawlins saddled Flame and headed for Beaumont, leaving the others to follow with the pack mule at a more leisurely pace.

When Rawlins reached the site of the pipe line operations, although it still lacked more than two hours until dark, he found the workings deserted. Tools were scattered about, as if they had been dropped hurriedly, but of the workers there was no sign. He pulled up in surprise, glancing about for some clue to the mystery.

To the west, not far distant, was a thick belt of chaparral that extended north and south for several miles. To the east the prairie was open for some five or six hundred yards, after which it was dotted with thickets and groves. Nowhere did anything move, and the silence remained unbroken. The late afternoon sunshine shone peacefully, and the faint breeze turned the prairie grasses into long ripples that gave the impression of approaching shadows although there was not a cloud in the sky. Rawlins shook his head and rode on, experiencing a certain disquietude. The men should have been at work for another hour at least. He quickened Flame's pace and soon was approaching the outskirts of Beaumont.

Arriving at the stable, he made sure all the sorrel's wants were cared for, then set out for the Alhambra; he had a feeling that Jason Abbot would be waiting for him there.

He was right. Abbot was seated at a table, a drink in front of him, and plainly in a very bad temper.

"Thought you'd be in this evening," he grunted as Rawlins occupied the opposite chair.

"Something wrong?" Rawlins asked.

The sapphire splinters that were Jason Abbot's eyes sparkled angrily in his leathery face.

"There is, plenty," he growled, "and something's got to be done about it, fast. Happened this afternoon not long after we'd knocked off for noonday snack. Somebody over to the east of where we were working started shooting at us. No, nobody hurt, but those slugs came mighty close. Naturally, the boys ducked and scattered. The shooting stopped, but when they started to work it began again, same as before, only the slugs came closer; one actually knocked a shovel out of a jigger's hand. The boys sort of panicked, and you couldn't blame 'em. Most of them are from the cities and not used to such shenanigans, and they're paid to lay pipe, not to eat lead. I figured the best thing to do was pull them off the job and hustle them back to town, which I did in a hurry. Nothing more happened."

"I see," Rawlins remarked quietly. "So they've resorted to that form of intimidation."

He sipped the drink a waiter brought him, rolled a cigarette and smoked in silence for some minutes, while Abbot watched him expectantly.

"Well, I think I can take care of *that*," he said at length. "Round up your men and have them on the job in the morning same as usual. Tell them for me that they won't have anything to worry about; I'll take care of it."

Abbot still looked expectant, but Rawlins said no more.

"If you send the word everything will be all right, they'll believe you," the oil man said at

128

last. "Okay, I'll have 'em out in the morning, but I've a feeling there'll be fireworks."

"There will be," Rawlins said grimly, adding, "And I've a notion you'll enjoy the display. I'm going to have something to eat; then I've got a ride ahead of me. Don't worry, Jason; everything will be okay."

"I hope so," the oil man replied morosely. "This business is getting on my nerves."

Rawlins ate in leisurely enjoyment, had a drink and smoked several cigarettes. For a while he conversed with Abbot on matters pertaining to the project, then got up and left the saloon. Ten minutes later he was riding swiftly toward the Lazy V ranchhouse.

The pipe fitters were punctually on the job the following morning. It was a bright sunny day with just enough frost in the air to set the breath to smoking. The men were tense, which was not unnatural, but, confident that Rawlins would not let them down, were in a cheerfully expectant mood.

"He's the bye to depind on," declared a big Irish foreman. "I'm after thinkin' some spalpeens are due to get a surprise they won't like at all, at all."

The others nodded agreement and picked up their tools. But barely had they started to work when four or five bullets whined past, close. Over a thicket better than five hundred yards to the east, keen eyes could detect a widening swirl of whitish smoke. The workers dropped their tools and dived for the shelter of the nearby chaparral. And from the chaparral belt tore more than a dozen riders, spaced out in open order.

It was the Lazy V outfit, mounted on the best horses their big remuda could provide. Straight for the thicket they raced, rifles flaming.

"Don't you go gettin' any fool notions and sashay ahead of us on that yellow devil," Zeke Pettigrew, the range boss, shouted warningly to Rawlins. "You'll just get blowed from under your hat; we've got to stick together."

From the thicket came a few answering slugs that whistled overhead. Then half a dozen horsemen burst into view and fled wildly south by east. The Lazy V cowboys whooped triumphantly and thundered in pursuit, gaining a few yards.

"We're doing it; hold your fire till we're closer," Rawlins shouted.

"After the snakes!" bellowed Pettigrew. "Meat on the table boys!"

Slowly the waddies closed the distance. The drygulchers knew they were riding a losing race; the white blurs of their faces showed as they twisted in their saddles to glance back at the fate that was steadily overtaking them.

Rawlins estimated the decreasing distance to the quarry. He waited a few minutes more, then shouted:

"Let them have it!"

The cowboys opened fire; a ripple of flame ran along their extended line; the air quivered to the reports.

One of the drygulchers spun from his saddle as if jerked down by a mighty hand. Another lurched sideways and thudded to the prairie. The cowhands howled like exultant wolves and redoubled their fire.

A few minutes later there were two more "good" outlaws. A fifth man fell. The lone survivor bent far over his horse's neck to provide as small a target as possible. To no avail. Another moment and he, too, leaned against the hot end of a passing slug. The cowboys pulled up. No sign of life was left save the riderless horses careening off across the prairie. Zeke Pettigrew wiped his streaming face with the sleeve of his shirt.

"Well, guess that's about it," he observed. "The buzzards won't go light-bellied today. Let's have a closer look at the skunks.

"These sidewinders always run to a common pattern," he growled a little later. "Big or little, there's the same brand of orneriness on 'em. Well, we've cleaned out this nest, anyhow. I'm pretty sure I've seen some of them hanging around Beaumont saloons."

Others were of a similar opinion, but that was as far as recollection went.

"Might as well be getting back to the diggin's,"

Pettigrew said. "Bet Abbot already has his boys on the job."

Abbot did have. The workers raised a cheer as the troop drew near, then bent to their tasks, singing and laughing.

"I've a notion that from now on whoever is back of this hellishness will have trouble hiring gents for their drygulchings," Rawlins told Abbot. "And from now on there'll be half a dozen or more of the boys riding patrol every day. I predict you won't have any more difficulties between here and Port Arthur."

"Suit me just as well if we do have," Pettigrew said cheerfully. "I ain't had so much fun since my mother-in-law got her nose caught in the clothes wringer."

Fourteen

Two nights later there was a stormy meeting in Jules Loche's rooms in the Crosby House. Loche was there, and Crane Francis, and two men Loche addressed as Bass and Ware. Marion, as usual, served the drinks and kept in the background.

"There's no two and three about it, Rawlins has us licked," Loche declared. "We've showed we can't deliver, and the pipe lines are going through. As a result, I've failed to negotiate exclusive agreements with the Gulf shippers. They'll take all the oil we can send by steamer, barge and the railroad, but that's as far as they will go. They refuse to boycott the pipe lines. Say they don't want to get embroiled in a feud with Gates and the Hogg-Swayne interests. That's what they say, but Rawlins is the real reason. It's *him* they don't want to get mixed up with."

"Can't blame them overly much," observed Francis. "Rawlins is a salty proposition."

"How about dynamiting the lines now and then?" suggested Bass, a lanky, saturnine-looking individual with a cast in one eye.

"That would only have nuisance value and mighty little at that," replied Loche. "It would just cause them some aggravation and get some more men killed; those lines will be patrolled so long as there's any hint of trouble, you can rely on that. All we can do at the moment is sit tight and see what that young devil's next move is; I'll admit I'm worried as to just what it might be."

"You don't think—" Francis began.

"I don't know what to think," Loche interrupted morosely. "He's as full of surprises as a grab bag, and he seems to have an uncanny ability to anticipate our moves. I wouldn't put anything past him, but I sure wish I knew what he has in mind." He whirled on his daughter.

"Marion," he said, "it's up to you to find out. Can't you do anything with him? I've never known you to fail yet when it comes to twisting a man around your finger."

"I'll try, but I haven't had much luck so far," the girl replied. She glanced at Crane Francis as she spoke. Francis smiled, his slow, lazy smile that never quite reached his eyes.

"When do you figure to see him again?" her father asked.

"I hope tomorrow night," she replied. "The last time he was here he said he expected to show up Friday, and that's tomorrow."

"Okay; do what you can," Loche growled. "We're depending on you. Come on, you fellows; let's go down to the lobby."

Rawlins had visited Marion Loche a couple of times during the past two weeks. He had found her charming, vivacious and companionable; but once or twice he had sensed a queer restraint in her attitude that puzzled him a bit. Always, however, it vanished quickly with her ready smile. He was inclined to regard it as a figment of his own imagination. She was good company and he liked her, but he was careful to keep their conversation on a strictly impersonal basis, although she seemed genuinely interested in his affairs and his plans for the future. About the first he talked freely, but was reticent where the second were concerned; he was not yet prepared to take anybody, even an attractive woman, completely into his confidence. Marion was all right, but, so far at least, she was but an incident in his life.

The evening of the conference in Jules Loche's rooms, Rawlins paused at the Alhambra for a snack. Audrey came over and sat at the table while he ate. He noted an unwanted listlessness in her manner.

"What's the matter?" he asked with an anxiety that surprised himself. "Something wrong?"

"Oh, I guess it's just that I'm cooped up too darned much," she replied. "I'm not used to spending twenty-three of the twenty-four hours inside."

"How'd you like to go for a ride with me tomorrow?" he suggested impulsively.

"I'd love it!" she answered. "Tomorrow's my day off."

"That's perfect," he said. "We can ride down to the southwest, circle around and make the Lazy V ranchhouse by dark. Uncle Rod will put us up for the night."

"Wonderful!" she agreed. "That is, if you don't think he'd object to offering a dance floor girl the shelter of his roof."

"Rats!" he scoffed. "Roderick McArdle wouldn't refuse a stray dog or cat a night's lodging; he's that sort. Oh, the devil! I didn't mean that the way it sounded."

She laughed merrily. "Of course you didn't," she said; "you don't need to look so contrite. You are just afflicted with the prevailing masculine genius for putting your foot in your mouth whenever you open it in the presence of a woman."

Rawlins gritted his teeth and changed the subject. "We'll start about noon, if that's all right with you," he said. "Where'll you meet me?"

"I know where you stable your horse," she replied. "I'll meet you there."

"Fine!" he agreed, adding doubtfully, "Perhaps I can rake up a sidesaddle for you."

"Sidesaddle, nothing!" she exploded. "I ride like a man. And don't go raking up some ambling old hack for me, either; I want a horse that is a horse. I can ride."

"Okay," he chuckled. "If I have to haul you out of a cactus patch, don't blame me."

"You keep yourself out of cactus patches and

don't worry about me," she returned composedly. "See you tomorrow; I've got to get back to work. Francis is liable to show up any minute now—he's been gone most of the evening—and he's got an eagle eye for loafers. Oh, I'm not complaining; he's got a right to ask his money's worth."

"He seems to be out a lot of late," Rawlins commented.

"Yes," she answered. "I've a notion he has other interests that are becoming more important to him than the saloon business."

There was a peculiar expression in her big eyes as she said it. Rawlins looked expectant, but she merely nodded goodbye over her shoulder as she sauntered back to the dance floor.

She met him the following noon at the stable, as promised. He regarded her admiringly. He had feared she'd show up in some outlandish riding habit, such as was approved by Miss Lucretia Sadler's Finishing School for Young Ladies.

She didn't. She wore faded Levis, well scuffed little spurred boots of softly tanned leather, a gray flannel shirt open at the throat—and a battered "J.B." perched jauntily on her reddish curls.

"You look wonderful!" he exclaimed.

"Thank you; I'm glad you approve," she answered, a touch of color in each creamy cheek. Her eyes met his honestly, and he knew she meant it.

"You're full of surprises, as always," he chuckled. "Wonder what next you'll have in store for me."

"You will be really surprised when you find out," she replied. "Oh, what a beautiful horse!"

He did not tell her that he had ridden down to the field that morning to borrow the splendid black from Jason Abbot's own prized collection.

"Glad you like him," he said. "He's not quite up to old Flame, but he doesn't miss by much. All set?"

She handed him a small parcel. "Put it in your saddle pouch, and don't lose it," she admonished.

"What is it?" he asked with a true masculine lack of tact.

"Well," she smiled, "I believe you said we'd spend the night at the Lazy V ranchhouse; a girl can't sleep comfortably in overalls."

Rawlins' face turned the color of a healthy sunset and he said something under his breath that was not fitting for a lady's ears. He stowed the parcel and offered to hold the stirrup for her.

She laughingly brushed him aside and mounted lithely without assistance. The way she settled herself in the saddle told him she was not unfamiliar with a hull and banished all anxiety as to her riding ability. He forked Flame and they set out.

It appeared all nature had conspired to give them a perfect day for an outing. The sky was the

138

deep and tremulous blue that only a Texas sky in autumn can achieve. A soft hush brooded over the rangeland, which lay bathed in golden sunshine. The grass heads were amber tipped with pale amethyst, and in the moister hollows the bronze of fading ferns was visible.

They spoke but little, charmed to silence by the unearthly loveliness spread about them.

"I think," Audrey said at last, "not even the Garden of Eden could have been more beautiful."

"I've a notion the Garden of Eden is everywhere, for those who can see and appreciate it," he replied.

"Yes," she said softly.

They rode on.

Rawlins continually studied the terrain as they rode in a wide sweep to the southwest and back again toward the north and east. Finally, when the low-lying sun was shooting its level rays of reddish light across the rangeland, he pulled up on the crest of a low rise and sat gazing eastward with brooding eyes.

"What are you thinking about, Wade?" Audrey asked curiously.

"I'm thinking," he replied, "that once upon a time, millions of years ago, the whole topography of this section was reversed."

"Reversed?"

"Yes. What is now lowland beyond the oil field

and the river was once a chain of hills, much higher and more rugged hills than those to the west. They were not worn down by erosion, such as the hills to the west are experiencing. They were leveled by some tremendous volcanic convulsion and, speaking in terms of eons, leveled very quickly. I am speaking of the surface of the land. By the surface, I mean hundreds, even thousands of feet in depth. But below that depth, the original topography still obtains. Deep down in the earth, perhaps a couple of thousand feet or slightly more, the sedimentary rocks are sloped even as they were before the upheaval."

"And if that is so?" she asked in interested tones.

"If that is so—and I'm convinced it is, although I'm still not enough of a geologist to offer positive proof—somebody may be in for an astonishing surprise." He smiled. "I won't talk about it any more right now—I'll be called crazy enough a little later—but don't forget what I told you."

"I won't," she promised. He could see that she was very curious, but she asked no questions. Impulsively, he added, "Wouldn't be surprised if I tell you a lot more soon; hope you won't be the first to laugh."

The honest blue eyes met his. "I won't," she promised. "I'll just be thrilled and happy."

"Happy?"

"Yes, for your sake, for I know whatever you have in mind will be successful."

Her serene confidence in him strengthened his resolve to gamble all he had acquired on a hundred-to-one shot with the odds against him.

They rode on through the blue magic of the dusk, and the Lazy V ranchhouse came into view. Its lighted windows glowed warmly through the gloom, beckoning beacons to welcome the traveler with their promise of comfort and hospitality.

Old Roderick himself met them at the door. "Well! well!" he exclaimed in hearty welcome. "It's been an unco longish time since this wee hoosie knew the fragrance of a lassie's presence. Come in! Come in! A McArdle's hearth is always wide."

Roderick McArdle insisted on preparing a room for Audrey with his own hands. And he offered his arm with courtly grace when she turned to ascend the stairs.

"She's a bonnie lassie," he said to Rawlins when he came back to the living room. "Aye, a bonnie lassie, with the blue of the glens in her eyes and lips like the red, red rose. I like a lass with a touch of sunshine in her hair, and sunshine in her heart. Aye, a bonnie lassie."

Wade Rawlins was greatly pleased at McArdle's undoubted approval of Audrey. He wondered fleetingly if he would also have approved of Marion Loche.

At dinner, the cowboys were at first a bit constrained by Audrey's presence. But her charm and graciousness soon put them at their ease, and the evening meal was its usual hilarious affair. When the boys were back in the living room, Audrey remarked in low tone to Rawlins:

"Wade, no matter what you do or what you become, I think this will always be a part of you."

"Yes," he agreed soberly. "I suppose, after all, I'll end up following a cow's tail, metaphorically speaking, at least."

Somebody suggested a poker game in the bunkhouse.

"Go ahead, Wade," Audrey told him; "the boys want you. I'll stay here and keep Mr. McArdle company."

"And bonnie company she is!" chuckled old Roderick.

Fifteen

Rawlins was right when he predicted the pipe layers would not encounter further opposition other than that provided by nature. The work progressed steadily despite topographical difficulties, which increased as the project drove farther south. A group of Lazy V cowboys constantly patrolled the route, assisted by volunteers from spreads across which the line ran. With these alert guardians on the job, the pipe men had no fear of outside interference and concentrated on the business at hand. Ten days after Rawlins and Audrey spent the night at the Lazy V ranchhouse, the workers boomed into Port Arthur to the accompaniment of cheers from a large gathering present to witness the event.

Hardly was the last length of pipe screwed into place before Bet-a-Million Gates materialized with a roll of bills which he proceeded to distribute among the workers.

"You boys have earned a celebration," he told them. "Go to it!"

The workers roared their approbation, and when the final mopping up was completed, they "went to it," beginning a celebration that would be the talk of Port Arthur for some days to come.

"I'm staying at the Austin Hotel on Beaumont Avenue," Gates told Wade Rawlins. "When you're free here, I'll meet you there, in the dining room."

Somewhat to his surprise, Rawlins saw Jules Roche in the gathering of Port Arthur citizens who were present. The financier greeted him cordially and congratulated him on the successful consummation of the project.

"I have an office in the railroad building," he said. "Drop in on me some time; perhaps we'll be able to discuss something of common interest to us both. If you see Marion when you get back to Beaumont, tell her I'll be detained here a few days longer than I expected."

Rawlins promised to do so.

After making certain everything was in order before he dismissed the workers, who hurried off to start their celebration, Rawlins joined Bet-a-Million Gates in the dining room of the Austin Hotel. They ordered dinner and ate in silence. After finishing their meal, they settled back to talk.

"Well, you did it, despite the opposition," Gates commented.

"Yes, and for a time it was rather formidable opposition," Rawlins replied. "What do you know of the opposition, if anything?"

"I've been nosing around a bit and I've learned this much," Gates said: "that Jules Loche has been trying desperately to tie up the Gulf shippers with agreements to move only oil that passes through the hands of the interests he represents. For a while he was making headway, for after the steamer explosion at Beaumont, the combine, as we call it for want of a better name, just about controlled the river boats. But when the pipe line started, the shippers pulled back and decided to wait and see what happened. If the pipe line had been stopped, I think they would have signed, and we would have had to pay through the nose to move our oil."

"Who are the interests Loche represents, do you know?" Rawlins asked.

"From what I've been able to learn, they are an eastern syndicate, and a very unscrupulous syndicate," Gates explained. "We have that kind in this country, you know, the sort who shut their eyes to what their field men do and disavow any connection with them if there's a slip and something really bad shows up. Usually they get away with it, too, for it is almost always impossible to pin anything on them. They're the bane of legitimate business but very difficult to track down. They always have a bunch of smart lawyers on tap, have important political connections, and cover their tracks well. I haven't so far been able to ascertain the identity of this particular flock, but I'm working on it."

"And do you think that Jules Loche, as their

145

field man, is responsible for what's been happening here?" Rawlins asked.

Gates shrugged. "I'm not prepared to answer that, because I have no proof," he replied. "You must judge for yourself. What do you think?"

"I think," Rawlins answered quietly, "that back of Loche is a shrewder and much more dangerous man who pulls the strings and tells him what to do. In my opinion, Loche would never initiate what's been happening here. Possibly, indeed probably, he would go along with it or be shoved along, but he would not initiate it."

"What makes you say that?" Gates asked curiously.

"I really have nothing concrete on which to base the assumption," Rawlins said. "But I have met Loche a few times and he doesn't strike me as being the killer type; and whoever blew up that steamer and had lead thrown at me a couple of times definitely is."

"Do you think you are still in danger?" Gates asked, a note of concern in his voice.

"Possibly, but perhaps not so much as before," Rawlins said. "I've a notion that now the pipe line has gotten through, my nuisance value, in their estimation, has dwindled."

"Don't be too sure," Gates disagreed. "That sort of an outfit always looks askance on any up-and-coming young man who opposes them. They're just as ornery and dangerous as your

Texas badmen, but their methods are more subtle. Well, I have an appointment with some shippers; I'll be seeing you in Beaumont within a few days. Suppose you'll see Hogg and Swayne as soon as you arrive there? They'll want to talk with you. Would have been here today if so many interests hadn't interfered; they're busy rounding up more oil."

Rawlins rode back to Beaumont the following morning, for he was anxious to talk to Hogg and Swayne and their associates as quickly as possible. On the way he paused to inspect the pumping stations and was pleased to find that satisfactory progress was being made.

Hogg and Swayne agreed with Rawlins that it would be wise to start another pipe line without delay.

"It's important that we keep the Gulf shippers reassured," said the latter. "We've got them coming our way now, and we want them to continue. Shoving the original line through as you did was a lifesaver. If you'd fallen down on the job or had been unduly delayed, Loche and his crowd would have signed up a majority of them, sure as shooting. By the way, we've voted you a bonus, and we are prepared to pay you for the second million barrels Abbot now has on tap. You're doing pretty well by yourself, young fellow."

"And I hope you'll keep on," added Jim Hogg.

"I hope you don't go throwing everything away on some harebrained venture that looks good to you. Young fellows have a habit of doing just that."

Rawlins held back a grin as he thought what the former Governor would say if he knew just what he, Rawlins, had in mind. He managed to keep a straight face as he thanked both men for their kindness. Now, he exultantly realized, with a moderate bank loan which he believed he could arrange, he was ready to embark on his great venture. He would do so just as soon as the new pipe line was under way. The survey had already been run, and he knew Jason Abbot could be relied on to carry the project through to a successful conclusion. He would talk to Roderick McArdle, whom he was confident he could swing in line, and to Abbot. He was in a decidedly equable frame of mind when he said goodbye to Hogg and the others and headed for the Alhambra; he wanted to have a word with Audrey. The darned little baggage hadn't been out of his thoughts since the night at the Lazy V ranchhouse! Perhaps he'd better see Marion Loche soon; she might function as an antidote. He chuckled and pushed his way through the swinging doors.

Audrey joined him shortly. "Well, I understand you have been a very busy man," she said by way of greeting. "Nice of you to remember me."

"Might be nicer for my peace of mind if I could forget you," he growled.

She smiled demurely, but said nothing.

"See Francis is absent again," he observed casually.

"No, he's not here this evening," Audrey replied. She regarded him in silence for a moment, then apparently made up her mind to tell him something she had been debating with herself.

"Wade," she said, "there's something I think you ought to know. Francis has been in the company of Jules Loche a good deal of late; they appear to be working together on something."

"The devil he has!" Rawlins exclaimed, his eyes widening. "I wonder how he became associated with Loche?"

"I think you'll learn he became associated with Jules Loche several years back," she replied. "This isn't the first time they've worked together."

"Well, that's news!" Rawlins said. "Funny, I don't recall ever seeing Loche in here."

"And I doubt if many people have seen Francis at the Crosby House, but he goes there," Audrey answered.

"Perhaps his interest is in Marion," Rawlins hazarded with a rather forced smile.

"To Crane Francis a woman is just a toy with which to amuse himself, and to break when he grows tired of it," Audrey retorted. "You can rest assured that his interest in Marion, if he has one, is strictly superficial."

"How about Marion?" he asked.

"As to that, I'm not prepared to pass judgment," she said. "But Crane Francis is the kind of man who is very attractive to women of a certain type."

"I see," Rawlins replied slowly. "Then you don't believe Marion is the reason for his association with Loche?"

"Definitely not," she answered.

"Then what is the reason?"

"You may be able to figure that out for yourself," she said. "Frankly, I don't know for sure."

Rawlins regarded her in silence for a moment. "Audrey," he said, "how come you know all this?"

"A girl hears things in a place like this," she answered evasively. "I thought you should know," she repeated. "Incidentally, you'll be doing me a favor if you don't repeat to anybody what I've told you."

"I won't," he promised. "And I'm glad you told me; it's given me something to think about."

"I thought it would." She nodded. "Well, there goes the music; got to get back to work."

"Darn it! I wish you weren't working in this place," he grumbled.

"Why?"

"Because something might happen to you."

"It won't," she replied cheerfully, "but it's nice of you to think of it."

"Why shouldn't I think of it?" he demanded exasperatedly. "You're one of the best friends I have in the world."

"It's nice to be a—friend." There was a mocking light in the blue eyes. Rawlins swore under his breath as she moved away.

A great light suddenly dawned on Wade Rawlins; his lips pursed in a soundless whistle.

Rawlins had been sincere when he had told Bet-a-Million Gates that he did not think Jules Loche capable of initiating the acts of violence that marked the fight for control of the transportation of the Spindletop oil. But Crane Francis was! Rawlins believed Crane Francis capable of anything. Francis, not Loche, was the head of the combine, the man who gave Loche his orders and who did not stop at murder to achieve his ends.

Certain things that had been obscure before were now glaringly apparent. If anybody had been in a position to anticipate his moves, it had been Francis. More than once, he recalled, the saloonkeeper, under the guise of friendly interest, had casually asked questions. And his answers had been more revealing than he thought. For instance, Francis alone had known of his intention to ride to the Lazy V Ranch, presumably to spend the night there. And on his way back to town the following morning, a near ambuscade had been set for him, resulting in the death of the drygulcher instead of himself. He remembered, too, that the night before the attempt was made on his life as his men ran the survey line, Francis had discussed with him the terrain over which he expected to pass, commenting that just beyond was ground that might give the pipe layers trouble, since it was cut by ravines and wide dry washes.

He was so overwhelmed by the unexpected discovery that he got up and hurriedly left the saloon, to wander through the streets restlessly pondering the problem.

Sixteen

The next morning Wade ate breakfast at the Alhambra, then got the rig on Flame and headed for the Lazy V ranchhouse. The time had come for another serious discussion with old Roderick McArdle.

Arriving at the ranchhouse, Rawlins found old Roderick pottering about the yard; his greeting was warm.

"I hear you're doing mighty well by yourself, lad," he said. I'm muckle proud of you."

"And I expect to do a lot better before long, Uncle Rod," Rawlins offered as an opening wedge for what was to come. "I'll tell you all about it."

"First we'll have a snack and some steamin' coffee," decided McArdle. "I can always listen better on a full stomach. And how did you leave the bonnie lass?"

"She's fine; I was talking with her last night," Rawlins replied.

"Waste not too much time in talk," counseled McArdle, the burr more pronounced than usual, "for ye ken a lassie's mind is aye a kittle thing. And while ye talk, some braw and sonsy man may walk."

Rawlins grinned, and thought it best to let it go at that.

After they finished eating, they returned to the living room. Old Roderick filled and lighted his pipe with great deliberation. He regarded Rawlins through the blue haze of the smoke.

"And now, lad, what have you on your mind?" he asked.

Rawlins drew a deep breath and took the plunge.

"Uncle Rod," he said, "I want to drill a well on your south pasture."

"Hoot! toot! lad, but you're crazy!" exclaimed the astonished rancher.

"I don't think I am, Uncle Rod," Rawlins said.

"But all the experts agree there's no oil over here to the west," protested McArdle. "Fact is, a feller did talk me into letting him drill a well, about a year back, down in the southeast corner of my holding. He went down a thousand feet and better and had nothing but a dry hole to show for his time and money; he gave up in disgust."

"He didn't go deep enough. He should have gone down another thousand feet; perhaps more," Rawlins replied. "If there is oil beneath your land, and I am convinced there is, it will be found at a great depth."

"What makes you say that, lad?" McArdle asked.

Rawlins repeated, in substance, what he had told Audrey.

McArdle shook his bald head. "Sounds interesting," he admitted, "but it would appear the oil people's engineers differ with you, and they should know what they've talking about."

"Uncle Rod," Rawlins smiled, "there's a maxim among lawyers. It goes something like this: 'Beware the young lawyer with a book.' Why? Because he may have dug up some forgotten precedent or obscure statute that will knock the old-timer's carefully prepared case to smithereens. I'll paraphrase that. 'Beware the half-baked engineer with a notion!' His knowledge is exhaustive, and because of that he is not hampered by what appears to be proven facts. He's still inquisitive and wants to find out for himself. So he continues to peer and probe, and as a result may hit on something which more mature minds failed to perceive because they accepted what was seemingly conclusive and did *not* continue to peer and probe. I believe that's my case."

"It's a bit hard to follow you, but I think I ken what you mean," said McArdle, shaking his head. "But I greatly fear you'll lose all you have acquired if you insist on going ahead with such a loco scheme."

"I'm willing to gamble on it," Rawlins replied cheerfully. "I'm not asking you or anybody else to put anything in the venture. In fact, I wouldn't allow anybody else to put anything in it. I'll stand or fall on my belief, but I don't figure to take a tumble."

"The confidence of youth!" sighed McArdle. "Weel, weel, you're young, and if you fall it won't matter over much; still plenty of time to make another start. Okay, lad, I'll go along with you; you have my permission to drill your hole."

"And we'll go halves on what I produce," said Rawlins. "Let's have your paw on it, Uncle Rod. I want to be the first to shake hands with a brand-new millionaire!"

"You're cookin' your rabbit before you catch it," said McArdle. Nevertheless he shook hands.

Rawlins' next visit was to the Beaumont bank which carried his account, where he requested an interview with the president. When he was admitted into the president's presence he laid the case before him in detail. The banker, a corpulent and rather jovial-looking individual with shrewd eyes, put the tips of his plum fingers together and sat for some time in thought. Rawlins could see the wheels turning over. Undoubtedly the banker was impressed by his association with Gates.

"This is a rather unusual proposition, Mr. Rawlins, and twenty-five thousand dollars is a rather large sum," he said at length. "But you appear to be an up-and-coming young man, and highly respected in certain quarters; so I think I can safely say that the bank will grant you a short-term loan for that amount. Give my regards to Mr. Gates when you next see him. I met him once and greatly admire him."

Rawlins promised to do so. He thanked the executive and left the bank in an exultant frame of mind. Now he was all set to go ahead. Doubtless everybody would think him plumb loco, but they had thought the same thing about Columbus.

Jason Abbot did think so when Rawlins approached him. What was more, he said so, in no uncertain terms.

"There's not a thing over there to indicate oil under the land," he protested. "No salt domes, no kerogen shale, no surface seeps. Not even any salt springs, as far I know."

"Jason, you are not altogether right," Rawlins replied. "I've seen one salt spring and one kerogen outcropping there."

"Just a freak, and an awful slim sign to go busted on," Abbot snorted. "One salt spring! One kerogen outcropping!"

"My theory," Rawlins explained, "is that such surface indications were almost completely wiped out in the course of the great geological change I'm convinced took place here ages ago. Otherwise, I think there would be plenty of signs instead of an isolated indication that somehow survived the general surface transformation."

Abbot shook his head and indulged in profanity. "But it's your roundup, and you have a right to twirl your twine any way you please," he concluded. "If you hanker to go busted, okay. Sure I'll hire you a rig, and I'll give you my best crew to handle. When you bust through to China, let me know."

Swayne and Jim Hogg were also vocal in their criticism, but Bet-a-Million Gates merely grinned. Quite likely he also disapproved, on general principles, but Rawlins felt that the long odds appealed to his gambling instincts.

Strangely, it was the experienced drillers Jason Abbot sent along with the rig who were optimistic.

"This oil business is a mighty funny business," declared grizzled Tom Calahan, the head driller and foreman of the outfit. "You never can tell about it, and the craziest ideas sometimes turn out to be the best. I've a notion, Boss, you may have folks laughing out the other side of their faces before you're finished with 'em."

Audrey was enthusiastic when Rawlins outlined his venture in detail for her edification.

"You'll do it, Wade," she said, her eyes glowing. "No matter what people say, you'll do it. You're going to become the big man you've dreamed of becoming."

Her sweet confidence was uplifting, but he only said:

"I hope you're right, but I've a premonition that I'm in for some hard sledding before the chore is finished; things have been going altogether too smoothly of late."

"You'll do it," she repeated. "I know you will!"

Seventeen

Down on Roderick McArdle's south pasture, the engineer opened his throttle; steam hissed; a drum turned. The ponderous walking beam jigged; the cable slid smoothly over the pulley that topped the tall derrick. The heavy bit plunged into the ground.

Old Tom Calahan, the foreman, rubbed his hands together complacently as he watched the churning drill. He glanced up at the pulley, studied the walking beam, then dropped his gaze back to the drill.

"She's a good rig," he said to Rawlins. "I'd prefer one of those new hydraulic rotaries, but they're mighty expensive, and we'll make out with old hop-and-skip. Well, there's the first foot of the two thousand!"

Day after day, the ponderous drill slashed and tore through loam and clay and shale. It pounded on stubborn rock, cleaved its way through the resisting strata and sank deeper and deeper into the unknown fastnesses far beneath the sunlight and the clean prairie air. The walking beam jigged, the pulley creaked and the cable rose and fell, paying out more and more line. The cuttings were "spooned" out, the bore kept clean and free from obstructions. Twice in the first thousand feet the cable broke while the bit was hammering rock. There followed the slow and tedious process of fishing for the "tools." But eventually the downward drive was resumed. Such accidents were all in the day's work for the experienced drillers; they expected such things to happen and gave them little thought.

"Way past the thousand mark, and nothing real bad has happened," Tom Calahan remarked to Rawlins one evening. "Casings have been going down without trouble, and there've been no cave-ins to slow us up. We're doing it, Boss."

Rawlins nodded. Calahan's optimism was refreshing. He did not dampen the foreman's enthusiasm by mentioning the financial diffi-culties that were steadily looming larger. His capital was fast melting; soon he would be in trouble.

Jim Hogg and Swayne were pessimistic, but John Warne Gates only grinned and said, "Let's wait and see."

Cowhands from the neighboring ranches and townsfolk from Beaumont rode to the scene of operations to look things over. Among them were Jess Bass and Mosley Ware, who had attended the meeting in Jules Loche's rooms and who were two of Crane Francis' henchmen. While playing the role of casual sight-seers, they kept close watch on the progress being made and reported back to Francis.

As the well grew deeper and deeper and nothing happened, the pessimists gained the ascendancy. Among them was the president of the Beaumont bank which had granted Rawlins a short-term loan of twenty-five thousand dollars. The president, in fact, began to grow nervous. Jules Loche and Crane Francis learned of this with satisfaction.

"About time to make your move," Francis told the promoter. "I've a notion this is going to work out easier than we expected."

The days passed swiftly, too swiftly for Wade. Soon his note at the bank would fall due. Well, he'd have to ask for an extension. He really didn't anticipate any trouble getting it; the bank would hardly want to foreclose on a dry hole, which was all the well was at the moment.

It was a gray day when he rode to Beaumont to take care of the matter. The sky was one vast leaden arch that seemed to press down on the earth, and a cold wind blew out the north. Stripped trees waved their bare arms in the blast. Long lines of brown, curling leaves scuttled before the gale.

Wade was in a somber mood when he reached town. He stabled his horse and without delay headed for the bank.

The president received him cordially enough,

but when Rawlins mentioned the errand that had brought him to the bank, the banker's face became bland and he put the tips of his fingers together.

"Oh, yes, the note," he said. He drummed with his fingers on his desk and smiled slightly. "Well, Mr. Rawlins, I'm happy to say that the bank doesn't own that note any longer; we sold it a few days ago."

"You sold it!" Rawlins exclaimed. "I wasn't notified of the sale."

"We would have notified you before the note fell due, as a matter of courtesy," the president replied. "We are not required to do so, of course. Such a mortgage is negotiable and can be bought or sold or transferred without the signer being notified."

Rawlins nodded; the banker was right.

"Who bought it?" he asked.

The president put his fingertips together again; he gazed at Rawlins complacently.

"Mr. Jules Loche," he replied.

Rawlins stared at him. Abruptly he felt numb all over, and a bit dazed.

"Jules Loche," he repeated mechanically.

"Yes," said the banker. "You will have to see Mr. Loche about an extension. Doubtless he will be glad to grant it."

Rawlins nodded; he didn't trust himself to speak at the moment.

"Yes, you should have no trouble getting your extension," the banker repeated. "Mr. Loche is an agreeable gentleman and I'm sure he will be glad to favor you. Good luck to you, Mr. Rawlins."

Rawlins thanked him and left the bank. He still felt slightly dazed and his mind was in a turmoil. Only one fact was glaringly apparent through the fog that shrouded his brain: he had been beautifully outsmarted. He saw it all now. Loche and Francis were also convinced that there was oil under the Lazy V land and had schemed to get control of it. Well, they had succeeded; it was laughable to think of asking Loche for an extension. He had failed; that was all there was to it. He didn't have the money to pay off the note and he was hanged if he'd ask anybody for it. He'd just keep his mouth shut and take his medicine. As a financier he was very much of a joke. Dealing cards in a saloon or following a cow's tail were about his speed.

Mechanically he walked to the Alhambra for something to eat and a drink; he felt that he needed both.

Crane Francis was at the far end of the bar when he entered. He nodded affably, and Rawlins nodded back, for he had no intention of letting Francis know that he was aware of the conspiracy between him and Jules Loche. It seemed to him that there was a gleam of malicious amusement in Francis' eyes. Doubtless there was; quite probably Francis was feeling very proud of himself at the moment.

The dance floor girls were coming in when Rawlins sat down at a corner table. Audrey arrived shortly, spotted him and walked over to the table. She instantly sensed his mood.

"What's the matter, Wade?" she asked, sitting down opposite him.

Rawlins told her. He felt he had to talk to somebody, and Audrey would keep what he said to herself. She listened in silence till he had finished, her eyes never leaving his face.

"And just what does it mean?" she asked.

"It means," Rawlins replied, "that when I can't pay off the note, Loche will foreclose and take over my holding in the well and any others that may be drilled; those were the conditions covered by the mortgage."

"I see," she said. She leaned forward and placed her hand on his. It was a very small hand with tapering fingers and beautiful almond-shaped nails.

"Wade," she said earnestly, "don't worry. Everything will work out so you'll come out on top. By the way, this is the twenty-third of December, isn't it? I want to be sure."

"Yes, it's the twenty-third, two days before Christmas," he answered. "Wonder what kind of a present I'll get?" he added bitterly.

"You may get one that will greatly surprise

you," she predicted. "I've got to go on the floor now, but don't worry; everything will work out."

His gaze followed her lithe little figure as she moved to the dance floor.

Eighteen

Roderick McArdle had asked Rawlins to spend Christmas Eve with him and share his Christmas dinner. Rawlins felt he could hardly refuse to accept the invitation. He grimly determined that he would do nothing to mar the festive occasion and pretended a lightness of spirits which he did not feel. It was around noon on Christmas Day when he left the ranchhouse and returned to Beaumont. After stabling his horse, he headed for his room to shave and clean up a bit. As he entered the lobby the desk clerk called to him.

"A young Mexican—I've a notion he's a swamper at one of the saloons—left this for you, Mr. Rawlins," he said, passing Rawlins a sealed envelope. "No, he didn't say who it was from; just gave it to me. He didn't speak English very well."

Rawlins took the envelope, which was addressed to him in a handwriting that was unfamiliar. He tore it open and extracted the contents, a folded document which he unfolded.

Then the envelope dropped from fingers that had suddenly become nerveless and fluttered to the floor. He stared in incredulous disbelieve at what he held in his hand.

It was his signed note for twenty-five thousand dollars. Across the face of it was written—PAID IN FULL!

Rawlins turned to the clerk who, busy with his register, did not notice his agitation.

"You say you didn't know the fellow who brought this?" he asked, his voice shaking a little in spite of his effort to control it.

"Why, no, Mr. Rawlins," the clerk replied. "Never saw him before, as far as I recall. Little dark smiling fellow who ducked his head, handed me the envelope and said, 'You give *Señor* Rawlins, *si*?' and slid out. Not bad news, I hope."

"On the contrary, it is very good news," Rawlins replied thickly. "I wish I could find that fellow and shove him a handful of pesos."

He turned his back on the bewildered clerk and mounted the stairs, the canceled note clutched in his hand. He fumbled his key into the lock, opened the door and sat down on the bed. For a long time he sat there, staring in front of him with unseeing eyes, feeling like a condemned man who had unexpectedly received a reprieve. Who in the name of blazes was responsible for this act that had given him a new lease on life!

Bet-a-Million Gates was his first thought. He proceeded to hunt up the financier, and found him, as usual, in the lobby of the Crosby House.

But Gates disavowed any connection with the matter: "Didn't even know you owed money," he declared. "Maybe Hogg or Swayne, though I don't think so. Figure they didn't know you were in debt to the bank, either."

Hogg and Swayne, when he sought them out, were equally unproductive of results.

"But one thing you can rely on, young fellow," said the former. "Jules Loche never canceled that note to show his charitable good will toward you. I've a notion he's fit to be tied. I wonder how the devil he was persuaded to let that note be paid off. Somebody sure must have put the screws on him."

"Maybe your old rancher friend," Swayne hazarded. Rawlins shook his head.

"Uncle Rod didn't know about me owing the money, either," he pointed out. "And I saw him last night."

"It's a queer thing," said Hogg. "Evidently you have some secret admirer who came forward at just the right time. Take the blessings the gods bestow on you, and don't ask too darned many questions. The way things are working out for you, I'm hanged if I'm not beginning to believe you may be playing a straight hunch. Remember, we have first bid on anything you may strike."

Rawlins went out and walked around awhile in the bright winter sunshine. After a time he dropped in at the Alhambra. He didn't see Crane Francis anywhere, but Audrey was there, earlier

171

than usual and sitting at a table. He hurried over to her and poured forth the story of the astonishing happening.

"Audrey," he concluded, his eyes glowing, "we are going to win!"

"We?"

"Yes, we!" he exploded. "I've just realized that if I can't have you, I don't give a continental about all the rest! What do you think of that?"

"I think," she said, her big eyes dancing, "that it is just about the most unromantic proposal a girl ever got. Wade, you're something! If I wasn't so utterly crazy about you, I'd die laughing. So you'd really condescend to marry a dance floor girl?"

Rawlins gritted his teeth and glared at her. "I suppose I'll have to put up with this sort of ribbing all the rest of my life!" he growled.

"Yes," Audrey replied composedly, "I suppose you will."

The day before Wade Rawlins received his mysterious and most unexpected "Christmas gift," Jules Loche received an equally unexpected visitor. He was sitting in his Port Arthur office going over some figures when the door opened and a young lady walked in. She was a very pretty young lady, modishly and tastefully dressed, with amazingly large blue eyes and curly red-brown hair. Loche stared at her in astonishment; then his eyes widened with recognition.

"Audrey!" he exclaimed. "Where the devil did you come from? What are you doing here?"

"It really doesn't matter, my dear uncle-guardian, since I *am* here," Audrey replied. "In fact, I've been here, or very close to here, for quite a while now, keeping tabs on you."

"Keeping tabs on me?" he repeated dazedly.

Audrey sat down, uninvited, crossed her knees and cupped her round little white chin in a pink palm. She gazed at him steadily for a long moment. Loche appeared to find her gaze singularly disquieting. He fidgeted, gulped, seemed at a loss what to say, compromised by saying nothing.

"Yes, keeping tabs on you," she said. "You led me a merry chase all over the country, but I finally caught up with you. I've been in Beaumont for quite some time now, waiting."

"Waiting?"

"Yes. Do you realize what the date is?"

"Why, it's the day before Christmas, the twenty-fourth," he answered, blinking his eyes in astonishment.

"Yes, the twenty-fourth of December." Audrey nodded. "I came very near being a Christmas baby, Uncle Jules, as you may recall. The twenty-fourth of December is my birthday, and this particular twenty-fourth of December happens to be my twenty-first birthday. Beginning to understand now?"

"What do you mean?" he asked, his voice quavering a little.

"I mean, my dear guardian, that the days of spending another's money for your own benefit are over. Your guardianship is ended and an accounting is in order. Oh, I know all about you and your doings—I've had lawyers working on the case. I know that you have squandered my inheritance on your harebrained or crooked schemes. I understand there is something less than thirty thousand dollars left of what was rightfully mine. Thirty thousand out of a quarter of a million!"

Jules Loche wet his dry lips with the tip of his tongue, and there was a haunted look in his eyes.

"I meant everything for the best," he said thickly. "I thought I was investing wisely and hoped to make you rich."

A derisive smile touched Audrey's red lips. "Perhaps," she said. "But the fact remains, my dear guardian who was unfaithful to the trust bestowed upon you by my dead mother, I can send you to prison, as you very well know. The lawyers are just waiting for me to give the word to move against you." She held up her hand for silence as he was about to speak.

"But I don't particularly desire to send you to prison," she went on. "It would create quite a family scandal back home, would it not, and shock a lot of nice people who still think of you

174

as honest and respectable? So I'm going to let you escape what you so richly deserve—on one condition."

"One condition?"

"Yes. I understand you hold Wade Rawlins' note for twenty-five thousand dollars. I'm paying off that note in full, with interest. I want it—now."

"But," he gasped, "that will leave you practically penniless."

Audrey shrugged daintily. "That prospect doesn't frighten me," she replied composedly. "I've been penniless quite a few times in recent years, and I've always made out. But I don't think I'll be left penniless. I'm confident that Wade Rawlins will strike oil, just as you and Crane Francis are confident he will strike oil. Oh, I know all about your association with Francis, and the crooked deals the two of you pulled together. I know why the precious pair of you, and Marion, left Spokane so hurriedly, and about the Denver mining business, and other things. I think you made a mistake getting mixed up with Francis, my dear uncle. You are just a common thief, but Francis is deadly, as you are liable to learn to your sorrow before you are finished with him. Now I want that note."

Jules Loche glared at her, his face black with rage. "I ought to strangle you!" he choked.

"I wouldn't advise you to try it," Audrey

175

replied. "You've been out here long enough to realize what happens to a man who lays a hand on a woman in this section of the country. Quite soon, dear uncle, you would be very, very short of breath. Give me that note! And if Wade Rawlins hears a word of this, all bets are off and to jail you go."

Loche ground his teeth in helpless fury. He fumblingly got the document from a desk drawer and passed it to her, his hand shaking.

"Take it!" he fairly spat. "And bad cess to you!"

Nineteen

Rawlins went back to work with renewed energy. His confidence was contagious, and the optimism of the drilling crew increased. Two days later, Tom Callahan pointed with pride to a ponderous contrivance he had brought over from the field.

"There's the valve to cap her with when she comes in," he chuckled. "Figured it'd be best to be prepared, because when she does blow, I betcha she's going to blow like all get-out. That's the way with these deep borings; the accumulation of gas is mighty apt to be terrific. We're liable to have our work cut out for us, getting her under control." He paused, gazing across the prairie which was dotted with groves and thickets, and his eyes grew thoughtful.

Rawlins liked the big head driller and had taken him completely into his confidence; Calahan knew all about Francis and Loche and their conspiracy. Now Rawlins sensed he had something on his mind. It was not long in coming forth.

"Wade," Calahan said, "from what you've told me, I figure you've put it over on a mighty hard bunch. Looks like you've got 'em roped and hogtied, but don't be too sure. They may have a card or two up their sleeves yet, and be ready to play 'em in the way that'll hurt most. I've had a lot of experience with this sort of thing, and there's something bothering me."

"What do you mean?" Rawlins asked, although he had a pretty good idea what Calahan meant.

"I mean that it would be easy for somebody to slip over here some dark night and drop a bundle of dynamite down the bore," Calahan answered. "It would wreck the derrick and the machinery, rip the casing and cave in the bore—I've knowed it to be done—and all our work would have to be done over."

"And there'd be no money with which to do it," Rawlins added. "So what's the answer?" Again he anticipated the foreman's reply.

"I think," said Calahan, "that it would be a good notion for you and me and one or two of the boys to sleep here at night till we finish the chore, with somebody always keeping watch. The cook shanty is big enough to accommodate a bunk or two and blankets spread on the floor. Night comes down early this time of year, and it's always plumb dark before we get back to town. Nobody would notice that all of us weren't riding in. What do you think?"

"I think it's a darned good notion," Rawlins agreed. "I'll ride in each evening and then slip out again later; not much danger of anything being attempted before midnight, I'd say. And if I

178

didn't show up in town pretty regularly, it would be noticed."

The foreman nodded agreement. "I'll get blankets and stuff we need here tomorrow," he promised. "I'd sure like to catch the hellions trying to pull that trick."

"Me, too," Rawlins said grimly. "I have a few scores to settle with them, and that would be a good way to do it."

"Don't underestimate them, though," Calahan cautioned. "That sort is dangerous, and if we ain't on our toes we may come out the little end of the horn."

Rawlins didn't argue the point; Francis and his bunch had demonstrated that they would stop at nothing. A little mass murder wouldn't bother them.

So it was arranged. Each night Rawlins, Calahan and one or two others, the workers taking turns, slept and watched in the cook shanty. Rawlins was usually awake most of the night, for he could drowse during the daytime. Now and then he managed to snatch a few hours of sleep in the evening before setting out for the well shortly before midnight. The horses not in use were hidden in a nearby grove. And day by day the drill sank deeper into the earth.

Audrey, much against Rawlins' wishes, insisted on staying on at Alhambra.

"Those hellions must have noticed we're

mighty friendly, and they might suspect you've been passing information to me," he pointed out.

"Very likely they have," she admitted, "but there's nothing much they can do about it. Besides, I like to see Crane Francis writhe. He doesn't dare fire me and he doesn't dare say anything; it's delicious to watch him. And I might be able to pick up some more information that will be of value to you."

One day, Calahan drew Rawlins aside. "There's a couple of jiggers I got my eye on," he said. "Their names are Bass and Ware. I know them both by sight. They loaf around the Beaumont saloons and gambling joints. Never seem to do anything but always have plenty of money. They've sure been taking an interest in things down here. Been here a lot of times with the other sight-seers, especially of late. Maybe, being idle, they have nothing else to do, but it looks a mite funny. They 'pear to be checking on our progress."

"We'll be ready for them," Rawlins replied grimly. "Keep an eye on them, though, and if you get a chance, point them out to me."

There came a day when Calahan, after drawing up the tools and changing the bit, said to Rawlins:

"Down twenty-two hundred and ninety feet now, and we're pounding something mighty hard and tough. I got a mighty good notion it's the cap rock. Bust through that and she's in. I'll bet my life on it that she'll come in 'fore the week's out."

"And no trouble so far," Rawlins commented.

"But those two jiggers I told you about were hanging around today, along with a lot of others," Calahan said.

"Yes, I spotted them from the description you gave," Rawlins answered. "Unsavory-looking specimens, especially the gangling one."

"That's Bass," said Calahan. "I heard tell he's a distant relation to Sam Bass, the outlaw who was killed quite a few years back. Well, here goes the casing and the new bit, and we'll start jiggin' through the cap."

But the cap rock, if it was cap rock, proved stubborn. The drill pounded away, making slow progress. Calahan remained optimistic.

"That's always the way," he said. "Cap rock is a tough proposition. But I figure from the sound of the drill that it's getting thin. All we got to do is keep things under control for another few days and we'll be settin' on top of the world."

That night it happened. Wade Rawlins, watching at the door of the cook shanty, heard a faint patter, and knew it was the beat of horses' hoofs a long way off. He aroused his companions. They grouped in the shadow of the shanty, tense and expectant. At their feet lay a huge bundle of oil-soaked waste, with a match ready to hand.

The pattering grew louder, slowed, ceased

altogether. The watchers strained their eyes and ears.

The final approach of the wreckers was so stealthy that nobody saw them actually arrive. The first intimation of their presence was a tiny flicker of light at the base of the tall derrick that reached into the overcast sky. Tom Calahan touched a carefully cupped match to the bundle of waste.

A sheet of flame shot up, making the scene as bright as day, revealing three men grouped around the well head—Ware, Bass and Crane Francis. Bass held in his hand a thick bundle of dynamite sticks, the fuse already sputtering.

"Drop that—get your hands up!" Rawlins yelled.

For an instant the trio stood transfixed. Then Crane Francis drew and shot with blind speed. The bullet ripped through the shoulder of Rawlins' shirt, graining the flesh beneath. He jerked his guns and fired with both hands. The others joined in; the air quivered to the drum roll of reports.

Bass gave a stricken cry and fell. The bundle of dynamite with its sputtering fuse dropped from his nerveless hand and straight down the bore. Rawlins rasped a bitter oath; this was the finish. No matter how it ended, the hellions had achieved their objective.

Ware went down, riddled with bullets, but

Crane Francis crouched behind one of the massive derrick legs and answered the group shot for shot. The hand that held the gun was all that was to be seen of him, and the light from the flare was dimming.

From the depths of the earth came a sullen boom, muffled by distance; the dynamite had exploded. Rawlins ground his teeth and fired at the white blur of Francis' hand.

Echoing the report was an awesome rumbling that instantly increased in volume, became a mighty bellow like the roar of an unchained giant. The experienced Calahan recognized it for what it was.

"Run!" he yelled. "The charge busted the cap rock and the well's coming in!" He whirled and rushed away from the derrick; the others followed at breakneck speed.

Rawlins saw Francis leap to his feet and flee madly. He did not waste a shot on him. Like the others, Francis' only thought was to put space between himself and the terror raging up from the very foundations of the world.

With a thunderous blast, the column of oil shot from the bore, hurling tools into the air, knocking the floor boards to splinters, snapping the massive supporting timbers as if they were reeds.

The derrick rocked and swayed, leaned out of the perpendicular and rushed down. Its black shadow enveloped the fleeing Francis. Its tall tip reached out toward him like the hand of doom. It seemed to fall slowly, almost gracefully.

Through the terrific crash of the derrick striking the ground knifed a single scream of agony and terror. Then all other sounds were drowned by the mighty roar of the gusher.

Up and up soared the glistening column. It feathered out, broke. There was a pattering as of a million raindrops falling.

"We did it!" whooped old Calahan, dancing and capering. The others joined with a resounding cheer.

Once again, Spindletop was in!

The second and greater Spindletop strike is history; the wells are still producing, town!" Calahan yelled above the turmoil.

"Blount, fork your bronk and hightail to round up all the boys and everybody else you can. We'll have a job getting that thing capped."

"And tell the sheriff what happened," Rawlins added. "God! Francis must be just so much pulp!"

"Serves him right," growled Calahan. "He wanted oil, eh? Looks like he got a mite more than he bargained for."

Hours after daylight, to the accompaniment of cheers from the crowd that had hurried to the scene, the well was capped, the valve firmly anchored. Tom Calahan wiped some of the oil from his face, turned and gravely shook hands with Wade Rawlins. His reeking drillers clustered around with greasy grins.

"And you all own a share in this one," Rawlins told them; "you've earned it."

Once again a resounding yell split the air.

"Hurrah for the Old Man!"

And at that moment Wade Rawlins tasted the sweet savor of triumph.

After washing up a little and grabbing a cup of coffee, Rawlins mounted Flame and turned his head toward Beaumont. He still had a chore to do, and it was a pleasant one. It was time for a showdown with Jules Loche.

On reaching town, he stabled his horse and walked to the Crosby House. Before Loche's door he paused. A lamp burned within, its beams sickly against the daylight, streamed under the door; but no sound came from the room.

Rawlins knocked, but received no response. He knocked again, and waited. The silence persisted, a strange and ominous silence. He turned and descended to the lobby.

"Get your keys and come upstairs," he ordered the desk clerk. "Don't stop to ask questions; do as I tell you."

The bewildered clerk obeyed. He selected a key from the bunch he carried, thrust it into the lock and opened the door.

There were two couches in the room. On one lay Marion Loche; on the other, her father. In the stiffened fingers of each was clasped a small crystal vial, unstoppered. In the air hung a faint, elusive odor, as of crushed peach blossoms.

"Are they asleep?" quavered the clerk.

"I'm afraid not," Rawlins answered.

"They—they're dead?"

"I'm afraid so," Rawlins said. "Yes, it looks like trail's end, the end of a crooked trail; we'll make sure."

He approached the couch on which Marion lay and gently removed the little bottle from her clenched hand. Holding it well away from his face, he shook it; the odor of peach blossoms grew stronger.

"Hydrocyanic acid!" he muttered. "They were prepared." He carefully placed the bottle on a nearby table, turned and shoved the gibbering clerk from the room. He closed the door.

"Notify the town marshal and the coroner," he told the clerk. "No, there's no sense sending for a doctor. One whiff of that stuff and you're done for."

Mouthing and muttering, the clerk stumbled down to the lobby. Rawlins hurried to Bet-a-Million Gates' rooms.

Gates was in. "Well, well, how's our young millionaire?" he exclaimed. "You did it, son, you did it!"

"Yes, I guess I did it," Rawlins replied wearily. "Wait; I have something to tell you."

Gates whistled through his teeth as Rawlins related his grisly find in the room above. He shook his head sadly.

"Double suicide, eh?" he said. "They knew it was the end, that everything was coming to light, and couldn't face it. God rest their souls! Now tell me what happened down at the well."

Rawlins told him, in a tired and listless voice. Reaction was setting in, and his early enthusiasm was dead as ditch water. Gates sent for Hogg and Swayne, and a lengthy discussion followed. Finally Rawlins rose to his feet.

"I'm going to hunt up a bit to eat and then lie down for a few hours," he told them. "I feel as if I'd been dragged through a wet cactus patch and hung on a barbed wire fence to dry. I'll see you later."

When Rawlins entered the Alhambra, the place was crowded, and everybody appeared to be discussing the oil strike and the suicides. His entrance was the signal for cheers. He waved his hand in acknowledgement and glanced about in search of Audrey. She was not on the dance floor, although the rest of the girls were. Finally he located her sitting alone at a corner table. She did not wear her dance floor costume but a simple dress he thought very becoming.

"Yes, I heard about it," she answered the question in his eyes as he approached. "I've already made arrangements for the funeral."

"Made arrangements for the funeral!" he repeated her words. "Why should you do that?"

"Because," she said as he drew up a chair, "Jules Loche was my mother's brother, Marion my cousin." She smiled wanly at his astonishment.

"Before my mother died," Audrey resumed, "she placed her estate in Uncle Jules' hands and made him my guardian. Proper safeguards were not taken, for she trusted him implicitly. To make a long story short, he proceeded to dissipate my inheritance to promote his wild get-rich-quick schemes. He sent money regularly to put me through school and provide for me properly until a couple of years back, when the money stopped coming. I went to a firm of lawyers, friends of my late father, and an investigation was started and the truth learned. I set out to run down Uncle Jules. He gave me a merry chase, for he hopped about like a flea on a hot skillet. Of course I could have set the law on his trail and located him more quickly, but I preferred not to do that except as a last resort. I didn't desire a family scandal, and after all, he *was* my mother's brother and she loved him dearly. I just wished, if possible, to salvage something from the wreckage of what he had misused.

"Finally I got a line on him. I learned that he was in partnership with Crane Francis, who was an excellent engineer and thoroughly familiar with the oil business until he got to fingering other people's money and had to cut and run for it and hide. Francis, like you, was convinced that there was another and larger oil pool under the land to the west, at a greater depth, and schemed to get control of it. You got the jump on him, so naturally he didn't love you. He and Uncle Jules worked various cities together, with Marion tagging along and lending them a hand whenever she could he useful."

"What a combination!" Rawlins muttered.

"Yes, wasn't it? Francis and Uncle Jules did not let it be generally known that they were associated; they considered it expedient, I suppose. I tracked them to Beaumont and learned that Uncle Jules was dabbling in the lumber business, apparently with success. I decided to wait awhile and keep tabs on him and his activities before confronting him, for I was close to twenty-one, when his guardianship would cease."

"So that's why you started to work here, eh?" Rawlins commented.

"Yes," she said. "I got Francis to take me on as a dancing girl here at the Alhambra, which wasn't hard to do. My only fear was that Uncle Jules would come in sometime and recognize me, although I didn't think it likely. I was a good deal younger when he last saw me, and he would hardly expect to see me on a saloon dance floor in a very short skirt and extremely low-cut bodice; hardly in the Boston tradition. That's why, as you mentioned once, I always appeared to be watching for somebody.

"Well, you know the rest, or enough. The twenty-fourth of December I was twenty-one, so I visited Uncle Jules in his Port Arthur office. We had a little talk and came to an agreement. There wasn't much of my inheritance left, but enough for the purpose I had in mind."

A light suddenly dawned on Rawlins. "Well, I'll be darned!" he muttered. "It was *you* paid off that note!"

Audrey lowered her eyes demurely. "Yes, I guess it was," she said.

Rawlins stared at her a moment, then chuckled. "So it looks like you own a half-interest in the well," he said.

Audrey raised her eyes. "Who cares about that!" she said. "All I want is always to own a whole interest in you!"

Center Point Large Print
600 Brooks Road / PO Box 1
Thorndike, ME 04986-0001 USA

(207) 568-3717

US & Canada:
1 800 929-9108
www.centerpointlargeprint.com